BLACKJACK YOUR WAY TO RICHES

BLACKJACK
YOUR WAY TO RICHES

RICHARD ALBERT CANFIELD

A LYLE STUART BOOK
Published by Carol Publishing Group

Manufactured in the United States of America
ISBN 0-8184-0498-1

Dedication

*This book is dedicated to those readers who will
recognize a good thing when they see it, and who will
Blackjack Their Way to Riches*

Contents

LIST OF TABLES

Preface

Aside from the audacious pun in the title of this book, there's an incredible assumption: that it's not only possible to win consistently playing Blackjack, but that it's possible to get rich at the game, as well.

That's all true, *if the reader is truly able to completely understand and follow the procedures and techniques outlined.* To aid understanding, we've attempted to make the directions as clear as possible, organize the material as simply as possible, and present the whole of the book in an upbeat fashion.

But no matter what we've attempted, it does not follow that every person, in every walk or station of life, or of every mental capacity or psychological makeup will be able to follow the material and put it to effective use.

Therefore, we cannot guarantee or warranty in any fashion that any individual or individuals can be successful at playing Blackjack. And further, we can assume no liability whatsoever for any mishap, mischance or any losses incurred during anyone's forays into gambling.

It's really a two-way street: we don't want any part of anyone's winnings if he can do it, nor will we back any part of his losses if he can't.

There's really no magic or "luck" to winning at Blackjack over the long run, as this book clearly states. The system and manner of play recommended herein has resulted from billions of hands run on computers and a combined total of approximately 60 years of actual in-play experience by the author and contributors to this book. We can absolutely state that the strategies work for us, and for others who have used them.

But despite the fact that the very best information has been disclosed, we still know that not everyone will be able to follow our plan to its most beneficial result. Therefore, we've built in some safety check-points to try and insure against anyone becoming too optimistic too soon or without cause.

Thus, the book is designed to teach simple techniques which should be mastered before going on to more complex ones. Further, there are a multitude of warnings concerning exactly what skills need to be mastered and what type Blackjack games those skills will be effective against. All directions, warnings, cautions and admonitions should be taken literally.

There's an old story about a guy who was told he had to do two things to become a man: make love to a woman, and shoot a lion. He comes back a few hours later terribly bloodied and mangled. "Okay," says he, "now where's that woman I'm supposed to shoot?"

The point is to follow directions lest, in this case, your money gets mangled. And heed the warnings; they are there for your protection. For instance, start small and use winnings to play bigger. Check playing ability carefully at home before risking any capital. Understand the strategy and money management thoroughly before playing for keeps.

And remember that the casino environment can cause the best laid plans to flee the minds of otherwise rational and thinking people. After all, it should be obvious that the casino environment is *designed* to bedazzle the mind and make plans, budgets and clear-thinking disappear.

So don't be misled by the potential this book offers: you can win *only* if you have the skills, knowledge, capital and capabilities, *and can use those factors intelligently in actual play.* Impulsive behavior and hunches have been the downfall of many people in casinos. Don't let it happen to you.

You're about to get the information which has the *potential* of making you a consistent winner at Blackjack, but consider soberly these words of caveat and caution.

THE AUTHOR

and

Expertise Publishing Co.

Money alone sets all the world in motion.

Publilius Syrus

The world is his, who has money to go over it.

Emerson

A feast is made for laughter, and wine maketh merry; but money answereth all things.

Ecclesiastes 10:19

Nothing comes amiss, so money comes withal.

Shakespeare

There is nothing so degrading as the constant anxiety about one's means of livelihood . . . Money is like a sixth sense, without which you cannot make a complete use of the other five.

W. Somerset Maugham

The rich man has his motor car,
His country and his town estate.
He smokes a fifty-cent cigar
And jeers at fate.

Franklin Pierce Adams

How pleasant it is to have money!

Arthur Hugh Clough

Introduction

If you pay attention, you just might get rich. That's the most you can expect from this book and that assumes a few things.

First, what rich is. See if this qualifies: Rich is when you have $100,000 cash income annually. Rich is when you own your own $100,000 home outright. Rich is when you pay cash for whatever you like—new clothes, a car, a boat, first class travel all over the world—whatever amuses you, within obvious limits. Rich is when you are your own boss and owe no one anything. This book details how you can get into this category with limited capital.

The name of the game with this potential is Blackjack, or 21. It is played in Nevada casinos and in resorts all over the world for big money, and each game can be yours to reap profits from. You can do this now, today, even though many others before you have tried —and mostly failed—and even though casinos are aware many folk are trying to beat them all the time.

So, what can you do to cash in on this amazing bonanza? First, you must be of at least average intelligence and be willing to use that brightness to light your way through a series of simple and logical steps. Don't be alarmed; you probably expend more wattage right now at something else with not nearly the possible returns this book can pilot you to.

If you have questions, you just passed the first intelligence test.

No, this is not the first book on the market designed to teach how to beat Blackjack. It might be the last, however. For this book contains the Expert System, the system based on the secrets used by the four top professional Blackjack players in the world today. And the Expert System is so powerful, it not only enables you to gather up the money, but has tremendous safeguards which insure you should never be detected as you do so.

If you've had any exposure to other Blackjack systems you know how incredible that last statement is. For the other systems you've heard about do not live up to the claims of their sellers. And isn't it funny to note that almost all other systems are promoted as being so powerful that their originators (or borrowers) have been barred from active casino play?

That's no selling point!

How good can any system be which has an admitted failure-factor just about the time you get good at it?

You have more questions, like: If yours is so great why give it away for such a low price?

To understand the answer, you'll have to meet the contributors to this volume, three men and a woman, all of whom have made a great deal of money playing Blackjack, and all of whom can play anywhere today, and do.

Then there's me, the writer. I'm a pit boss and I've been working on the inside of Las Vegas gambling pushing 20 years now, mostly on the legendary Las Vegas Strip. Where the *real* action is.

That's not just pride, or cheap snobbery. Where I work, we get more action in a month than the casino at Monte Carlo gets in a decade. The restaurants in our hotel alone gross more bucks than most casinos in the world capture for their entire operations.

I can't give you too many personal details, as I like my position in this gambling world. But I'm going to enjoy telling the way gambling—and especially Blackjack—really is, and exactly how you can still get rich with the right information.

There's a lot of bad information being bandied about these days, hustled by people who claim to be "in." They are overdue for a surprise or two. I'm going to have a lot of fun unloading a tripleton of good stuff for the first time in print. It's going to make a lot of "authorities" squeal and dance.

You'll meet my contributors individually later—and listen and learn as they recount their experiences and techniques—but first, a few general reasons why they are willing to share the secrets of their success. Given the fact they are all human, the answers fall into logical and illogical areas:

LOGICAL

. . . All four have it made. Each has a net worth reputed to be between $285,000 and $3,700,000. They have all reached the point where they spend more time enjoying their money, or living off investments, than playing Blackjack.

. . . All four are moving more into part-time, but bigger money play as a result.

. . . All are getting the comfortable kind of lazy that comes with having a big financial cushion and sound investments.

. . . All four can afford to be a little tired of the game. Each has spent from five to 25 years at the "trade," and that's a long time in one slot, even if they *can* afford their own gold watches for faithful service.

ILLOGICAL

. . . Did you hear about the guy who climbed the highest mountain to get the secret of eternal youth from the guru? He got it under one condition: if he told anyone else it would no longer work. Imagine his excitement; now he would be eternally young, would know pleasures yet to be invented, would be rich beyond belief by merely putting $100 in the bank and letting it collect interest for 100,000 years. He would own the very world. The secret was so simple and beautiful he naturally went home and told his wife and three friends.

So call it the human desire to share, although these four professional players were wise enough to secure their own nest egg first before even considering sharing.

. . . Ego. Imagine their frustration at not being able to tell anyone of their accomplishments as one system after another hit the market, each with claims made for it more extravagant than the last. Imagine possessing diamonds and having the world admire costume jewelry. Imagine paying for an expensive computer run to compare a highly-touted system to your own, then finding the other vastly lacking in earning capability; or wading through an incredibly complex book jammed with charts and graphs only to discover that while the system therein is approximately correct mathematically, it is totally unworkable in actual play; or worse, to critically analyze a top-selling system only to find it completely absurd. Imagine rage at discovering ripoff artists pillaging a gullible public; imagine disgust at discovering rampant incompetence, however well-intentioned; imagine not being able to say:

"Hey, look! We can do it better, more efficiently, with a higher rate of profit and without being barred . . . look, ma, no hands. . . ."

If you can imagine these things, you can see it's illogical and all too human, but these pros resented having to suppress their egos while others got the glory for systems not nearly as powerful, successful or proven.

But don't imagine that these professionals were about to speak up until their own nest was well-feathered.

Now a question about me. Why don't I take the system and run? Don't forget, being a pit boss all these years has made me very well known. I have a reputation for knowing more than most folks about Blackjack system play. No one suspects how grateful I am that I never had a job depend on catching my contributors.

The problem with being respected as "sharp" means no one is going to believe for long that I'm likely to quit my job and play Blackjack full time just for fun. But don't get the idea I don't play at all. There are lots of places outside of Vegas I am virtually unknown, and lots of places here that are asleep.

But more important, I'm very secure and financially comfortable, and am now able to do many things I enjoy on the side—and make money at. This book is an example.

So why would these pros just turn over their fabulous system to me for whatever use I see fit, especially when they know I would both check it out very carefully *and* play it?

Basically, I've helped make all of them a great deal of money in investments, another sideline of mine. Too, we're all on good enough terms to ski and golf together. But also—another human quirk—none believes I have the gumption to go through the ordeal of writing a book, and none believes that readers would be able to tell the difference between a great system and mediocre ones, even if all the facts were presented.

So who said professional gamblers don't get trapped into making sucker bets!

You are now reading the book, and telling the difference between good and bad systems at a glance is easy, even without looking at the hard facts presented later on. Simply spend a minute or two looking at all the other systems you can get your hands on and you'll find they fall into three obvious groups: 1) Too confusing to work, 2) Too simplistic to be effective, and 3) Too complicated to apply in actual play.

Ignore for a moment that a few of the books easily fit into more than one category and that most of their authors have been barred for using their deficient systems. Now think: really top professionals in any field not only get it on effectively, but make it look easy in the process. That's what comes from knocking out frills and garbage and getting to the true, palpitating heart of the matter.

That's what you hold in your hands. You won't dazzle anyone with your footwork; you'll just learn to deliver the knockout punch.

Last question for now: Why don't casino personnel read this book and use its secrets to eliminate the threat to their bankrolls?

You'll find greatly detailed answers to this in the text—as you will also find answers to most of your other questions—but for now, the answer is: why should they bother to read anything but their profit reports? For so far, with every new system to hit the market, BLACKJACK PLAY AND PROFITS HAVE INCREASED. From a casino owner's viewpoint, what could be sweeter than that?

To get you in action as soon as possible, every effort has been made to eliminate the complexities, misconceptions and mystique which surround Blackjack, those elements largely perpetuated by system pushers who can't really beat any game away from their own living rooms. Have you noticed how the system hucksters challenge each other to "freeze-out" games for from $10,000 to $100,000 to "prove" who has the superior system? You'll find no such challenge in this book at those prices. As one of my contributors put it, "The system pushers have to play each other for peanuts. When we go out, it's to play against casinos that can have that much money at a *single table*."

Incidentally, don't be put off by all this big-money talk. We realize you might have bought this book without being particularly impressed with getting rich playing Blackjack. You may be doing satisfying and/or rewarding work right now and are only looking forward to paying for a Las Vegas or Caribbean vacation. Or you might want a little extra cash. Or you may simply wish to feel confident you are not making complete sucker bets and want to polish up your game for occasional gaming ventures. In other words, you might just want a piece of the action and not the whole pie.

Therefore, this book is organized to enable you to reach the exact point of powerful play you wish in the shortest possible time with the least possible effort. It assumes you have no exceptional skill and perhaps don't even know how to play Blackjack. It will take you through easy stages of added playing power, all the way to the top, if you wish.

And to help make that trip as speedy as possible, Blackjack Your Way to Riches has been organized with a keen eye to efficiency. If you read the text matter straight through, that will guide you along the quickest path towards winning—a straight line through the center to the goal.

> The boxes, like this one— *and in this kind of type–are designed to give you supplementary information, sometimes technical, sometimes explanatory, sometimes just fun. You'll usually find them at the tops of right hand pages.*
>
> *Combined, the text and the boxes present an extraordinarily thorough picture of Blackjack play.*

But for those who choose to be more casual in approach, just one quick skimming of this volume should eliminate dozens of potential sucker plays.

It's up to you and how far you want to go: take what you like, you'll like what you take from pros who have taken plenty.

Now meet these high-rolling pros who have agreed to share the results of their endless computer runs, their countless hours of experience which has culminated in the Expert System. They're an interesting lot, and I'm sorry you can only meet them by nickname.

GRINDER. He's been at it the longest, about 25 years. He's also made the most money, becoming the first millionaire in the group. He was once a mathematician and computer programmer. He claims he hates playing Blackjack but loves the money, which he continually pumps into investments. (Like the others, he considers Blackjack winnings as seed money for investments.) He has had a series of financial advisors who convinced him he needs drawers full of second mortgages and stocks and bonds of every sort. He has a small empire and a large ulcer, a result of the last dip in the stock market. He describes his situation thus:

"Those inept advisors keep telling me to put my money in this and that and somehow I keep listening. I keep asking myself, why? Last month I lost $86,000 in the stock market at a time I had hoped to be making money. I finally had to go back to Blackjack to get even. None of those bloodsucking advisors have any shame. I'm sure they'll have more advice for me shortly. If I keep listening, they'll have me playing Blackjack the rest of my life."

Grinder is like that. After any given Blackjack play he can't wait to rush out and invest his winnings. And when he's not doing that, he runs up and down Georgia cotton fields checking for boll weevils or through South American coffee plantations analyzing labor efficiency, all so he can invest intelligently in commodities.

He's been doing just about the same thing with his empire for the last ten years, is 48 years old, figures he could sell out all his investments and retire with about $3,700,000 cash, but can't wait for the next investment. He says he hates it, it's a terrible *grind* and he's sorry he ever saw a deck of cards. He is also the first to extensively analyze some minor rule change in, say, a small Bavarian casino, and then talk animatedly about it for hours.

HUNGRY. He has been at it about 20 years. He used Thorp's and every other system until by chance he became friends with two others in this group, and they chipped in to help pay for expensive computer runs which resulted in the Expert System. He's as delighted at beating 21 as Grinder is unhappy.

"When one of those joints adds on another ten floors, I like to think I'm the reason they couldn't add on an eleventh," he says.

What delights Hungry most about playing is the freebies, for which he has an endless appetite: comp (complimentary) meals in the gourmet rooms, free suites, gratis limousines. He says when he got his first million dollars (partly through sound investments of Blackjack cash) he decided he would go into semi-Blackjack retirement and limit himself to a few high-rolling plays in Vegas, London and the Caribbean, and then quit when they finally got onto him.

"They won't let me quit; they just love it," he says. "The word's out I'm a sucker, you know, and just lucky. So they keep hounding me and I have to take the best offer. I let them fly me here and there, comp a suite, a show or two, and maybe some duck with truffles. Then I play a few hours a day at a reserved table. The last day or so I throw back ten or twenty thousand just to keep their interest up, then I leave. You know, if they just weren't so friendly about it, I'd quit gambling."

PARTY. He's third in time at it, 10 years. He had the worst time keeping money because of an unfortunate desire to see if he could spend more impressing blondes, brunettes or redheads. Every time he resolved this question in all the countries in the world with Blackjack games, Clairol hit the market with more hair dyes and he had to start over again.

Now the party is over for Party. He married Grinder's daughter and it has changed his playing style considerably.

"I used to get all I could and retire until the money ran out . . . never thought much about tomorrow or going back. Now I'm more settled and want to take time to enjoy my new wife and the places we plan going and to stockpile the money. No more hit and run, and both of us are playing nice and easy so our separate piles keep growing steadily."

Party estimates he only has a couple hundred thousand put away, "but you should've seen what I spent."

MRS. MS. She is youngest, the only female and has played about five years. Grinder is her father and taught her the ropes.

Earning Power

If you'd like a sneak preview of the hourly rate you can win playing the Expert System, take a look at table 9 in chapter 4, "Money Management."

She is very serious, independent, liberated and likes to plan ahead.

"I decided I would have at least $100,000 in the bank before I'd consider marriage and getting tied down. Now I have more than twice that, and no longer feel marriage is a trap. A couple of years from now, Party and I are going to open a resort, settle on one of the islands and start populating it. Tourists will be welcome, cars will be barred and polluters drawn and quartered."

Mrs. Ms. believes more women could make big money playing 21 if they'd learn the game the right way and quit letting men tell them to go play the slot machines.

Incidentally, with the exception of Mrs. Ms., the nicknames we all agreed upon for my contributors all have a slightly negative tone in gambling circles. There's a good reason; each name denotes a distinctive psychological technique its bearer uses as a deceptive style, strictly for profit purposes. The mystery is cleared up in chapter 6.

Well, you know me, so that's the whole crew. At the beginning of each chapter you'll find excerpts of conversations we've had about Blackjack which are especially revealing. In chapter 6, my contributors take just about complete charge and tell you everything they know about Keeping Your Name on the Welcome Mat, plus many other goodies. You will be amazed at how relatively easy it is to become a winning player with pros like this helping you.

So pay attention. You just might get rich.

When the One Great Scorer comes to mark against your name—
He marks—not that you won or lost—but how you played the game.

Grantland Rice

Ill can he rule the great, that cannot reach the small.

Edmund Spenser

A mighty maze! but not without a plan.

Alexander Pope

Fortune may have yet a better success in reserve for you, and they who lose today may win tomorrow.

Miguel de Cervantes

1 Rules for the Game of Blackjack, or 21

Know your
ABC's well

Grinder:	*You believe you're going to teach people to beat 21, I'd say you better teach them how to play it.*
Party:	*Yeah; from what I see, most people don't even know the rules.*
Mrs. Ms.	*You aren't being fair. Most people gamble for fun and pick up the rules as they go along.*
Hungry:	*Maybe, but I'll bet my next free meal most never reach the point where they know how to take Insurance, or split pairs or handle Surrender, much less why or when.*
Grinder:	*What I'm saying is most people could have a lot more advantage if they knew the rules and how to make the most of them.*

After all these years as a pit boss on the Vegas Strip, not to mention a few more as consultant/boss in foreign casinos, it continually surprises me how many people chunk their money in at Twenty-One without really knowing *how* to play. And that includes many "high rollers."

Give this chapter a good going over to make sure you have all the rules down pat. Even if you're familiar with the basic game—and that's about the same everywhere—check that you're not passing up any available options.

Of course, knowing how to play and using that knowledge to get an edge isn't the same thing. So I'll make you a proposition: become intimate with all parts of the game, then I'll show you how to make each work to your advantage.

Number of Players

Any number between one and seven players play against a dealer. You can play more than one hand if the game isn't full.

The Pasteboards

Many casinos still use a standard 52-card deck of cards. However, the trend is towards multiple decks—either two decks or four shuffled together. Some foreign casinos use six or eight decks. Generally, multiple decks increase the house advantage slightly. With one and two decks, the dealer holds the cards in his hand; with more than that, he deals from a card-holding box called a "shoe."

Card Values

You add only the numbers on the cards; suits mean nothing. So, two through nine count at face value; Tens, Jacks, Queens and Kings all count as 10. The only tricky one is the Ace, which counts as either one or 11, at your discretion.

Your Objective

You try to achieve a card total higher than the dealer's without exceeding a total of 21. You play individually against him, as if only you and he were playing.

Naturals—The Name of the Game

If your first two cards consist of an Ace and a 10-value card (including face cards) you have a Natural, or Blackjack. This is sweet. You automatically win and are paid 1.5 times your bet ($15 for a $10 bet, say). That is, you win unless you're unlucky enough to have the dealer also get a Blackjack on the same hand. Then it's a stand-off and no money changes hands. Note also, if the dealer gets a Natural and you do not, he gets no bonus, so all you lose is the amount you bet.

Game of the Name

Not many years ago Blackjack had such regional names as, Vingt-et-un (France), Ein-un-Zwanzig (Germany) or Van-John (Australia), and the rules varied considerably. These days, you can put your money up in almost any casino in the world while requesting "Blackjack," and you've got a game with only minor changes in rules.

The Blackjack Table

A Blackjack table is shaped somewhat like half of an apple pie. The objective of the game is for you to get some of the goodies which tend to gravitate towards the center of the pie, in the money tray in front of the dealer.

If you divide this half-pie into about seven slices, you will have the approximate number of positions for players a table can accommodate, though a single player can bet in more than one sliced position if no one else is already betting there.

Oddly, the farthest position to your right, as you approach the table, is called "First Base." And the farthest position to your left is called "Third Base." There are no other baseball terms whatever associated with the game.

But maybe this brief description explains Blackjack's popularity: it's as American as baseball and apple pie.

Betting

Before the deal you signal your intention to play by placing your bet in the betting space, usually a rectangle or circle painted on the table layout.

Betting Limits—The Mini-Max

Each casino sets its own betting limits, establishing both a minimum and a maximum bet. Limits often vary from table to table and from casino to casino.

Most Nevada casinos allow you to bet from a $1 or $2 minimum to a maximum of $500. Larger casinos often set aside a few tables with a higher mini-max, say, $5, or $25, or even $100 minimums and $1,000 or more maximums. The high rollers hang out here.

Each table usually has a small plaque stating the mini-max,

unless it has the standard $1 or $2 minimum. Check with the dealer if in doubt.

Shuffle, Deal, Action

The dealer shuffles and a player cuts. The dealer then "burns" a card—takes the top card out of play by placing it face up on the bottom of the deck or putting it into a discard box. Each player bets. The dealer then deals one card face down to each player clockwise and gives himself a card, face up. In the same way, he gives each player a second card and this time takes his own face down, sliding it underneath his first card (the one you can see is called his "upcard," the one you can't, his "hole card").

That's how it goes in single deck games. In multiple deck games, your cards may come to you either face up or face down, depending on house policy. The dealer, of course, always gets his second card face down. But since he must play according to rigid rules, whether or not he can see your cards in no way influences his play.

Hard, Soft and Breaking Hands

If your hand (your cards) contains an Ace which can be valued as an 11 without causing the total to exceed 21, you have what's called a "soft" hand.

All other hands—besides Naturals—are called "hard" hands.

Additionally, if you have any hard hand totaling 12, 13, 14, 15 or 16, then you have a "breaking hand," or more colorfully, a "stiff."

Keep in mind you will learn how to get a big advantage by sometimes playing soft hands differently than hard hands of the same total value.

The Draw, or "Hit Me"

If the dealer doesn't have a natural he again proceeds clockwise to players who in turn elect to "hit" (draw additional cards one at a time) or "stand" (take no cards). You lose your bet immediately should your cards exceed 21, as for instance you hit a total of 15 and receive a 9 hit card.

The dealer takes his turn last and starts by exposing his hole card. He stands or draws according to very precise rules: if his

---

A Game Played by Mutes?

Many experienced players never say a word when they play Blackjack, sometimes for hours. They indicate all their decisions for play by a succession of hand motions, gestures and signals. When they want to stand pat, they silently push their cards under their bet. They indicate a draw by scraping with their cards. They indicate a busted hand, a double down or a split by turning their cards face up and making the appropriate move with their money. In face-up games, they'll motion with their hand for a hit, hold up their hand for a stand.

With a table full of these silent, gesturing players, the game runs quickly and with lackluster efficiency. After a long while, if someone says something, it often kicks off a rush of chatter while players discover their voices again.

Bulletin To Casinos

Watch out when you're gettin' all you want. Fattened hawgs aint in luck.

Joel Chandler Harris

---

total is 16 or less, he *must* draw until he has a total of 17 or more. Then he must stand. If his hand contains an Ace, he must value it as 11 if it brings his total to 17 or more without exceeding 21. Note though, that some casinos modify this rule and require dealers to hit *soft* 17 but stand on soft 18.

Final Settlement—Win, Lose, Push

If the dealer hits and goes over 21—whoopee! He now pays all players who haven't previously gone bust an amount equal to their bet (Naturals are usually decided earlier). If neither player nor dealer bust, the one with the higher total wins. Anyone who has the same total as the dealer (not exceeding 21) has a tie, called a "stand-off" or a "push"—no money changes hands.

After settling bets, the dealer either gathers up the cards used in the last hand and deals another from the unused cards, or shuffles all the cards and deals again. If you want to stay in the game you make a new bet and the process starts over.

Splitting Pairs

If your first two cards are numerically identical you have a pair. If you wish, you can separate these and use each as the nucleus of a new hand—separate them face up on the table, put your original bet by one of the two cards and place an amount equal to that by the other. After splitting, you are now playing two different hands; you draw and complete the first before drawing to the second. Some casinos let you double down after you receive the second card on either split hand.

If you split and your first draw to either is another card of the same value, you can split again in most casinos. However, Aces are handled differently: you cannot re-split and you only get one card on each, usually face down.

Also, should you get a 10-value card on a split Ace, this is not considered a Blackjack but only as a total of 21. The same is true in splitting tens (*generally* one of the worst sucker bets around): should you get an Ace you only have a total of 21 and don't get the 1.5 times bonus.

Doubling Down

In Vegas you can "go down for double" on your first two cards, regardless of the total. You simply turn your cards face up, push out an amount equal to your bet, and the dealer will give you one more card, usually face down. This "doubling down" varies widely throughout the world. For instance, in Reno and Lake Tahoe you can only double on a two-card total of 10 or 11; in some French casinos you can't double at all.

Be sure and ask; the less you can double, the greater the house advantage.

Insurance

When the dealer's upcard is an Ace, most casinos allow you to make this additional wager. It's a simple proposition; if you think the dealer has a 10-value card in the hole, and therefore a natural Blackjack, you push out any amount up to half your original bet before he looks at his bottom card. If he has a Natural you win two times the amount of your side bet. If he doesn't, you lose the side

---

The Comfy Game

Blackjack is the most comfortable game to play in any casino. You get to sit down, unlike craps. You don't have to reach far or crane your neck to play, as you do in roulette. You can also talk casually to other players and to the dealer, all of whom are more relaxed than at other games.

The house will also keep you supplied with cigarettes and with enough drinks to keep your judgment impaired.

For most people that's too comfortable. Instead, ask for soda pop, orange juice, coffee, tea or milk.

And if you're the only person in the house playing $100 chips, order yogurt blended with fresh fruit and wheat germ. If they have to, they'll send a cab across town for it.

Options, Options, Options

Part of the fun of 21 is using the options which are a part of the rules to your advantage. It's a game of "sometimes-you-do" and "sometimes-you-don't." For instance, though you can draw to any hand you get, sometimes you will and sometimes you won't. The same for doubling down . . . you may or you may not. And pair-splitting gives additional choices: you can split and play two hands; or you can stand, hit, or possibly double down.

Playing these, and many other options correctly, is the way you whittle down the house percentage against you. And the real joy of Blackjack is knowing you are taking the rules and options the other guy made up and are using them to beat him at his own game.

Read on and enjoy.

---

bet and play continues. Regardless of the side bet, your original bet is won or lost in the usual way.

For example, suppose you make the side bet equal to half your original wager; the dealer has a Blackjack and you do not. You lose your original bet but get paid 2 to 1 for your side bet and break even on the whole transaction. Hence the name, "Insurance."

Now suppose you both have Blackjacks: you get paid 2 to 1 for your side bet and the Blackjacks are a push with no loss to either side on your original bet. This seemingly attractive outcome prompts many players to insure against an Ace when they have a

Blackjack themselves. You'll see why later, but for now never take Insurance unless you are keeping track of cards. Take my word.

Surrender

A few casinos offer this and when you know how and *when* to use it, you can use it to nice advantage. It works like so: if, when you get your first two cards, you decide the dealer is a cinch to win, you take back *half* your bet and throw in your hand without playing it out. It only sounds bad—sometimes you'll *know* that half of something is better than all of nothing.

RULES WE WILL PLAY BY

In order to make this book clear as possible we'll assume a set of rules. We'll stick to an average Vegas set for two reasons: 1) there are more Blackjack tables here than anywhere else in the world, 2) when you've mastered our system you'll want to come haul away a few stacks of the horrendous piles of money lying around here.

Our rules:

. . . You can double down on your first two cards regardless of total.

. . . You cannot double down after splitting pairs.

. . . You can split any pair and re-split all pairs except Aces.

. . . You can take Insurance.

. . . Dealer must hit 16 and under and stand on all 17's, including soft 17.

. . . You play using a single deck.

For now, don't worry about how various rules and conditions affect the house percentage against you. In chapter 5 you'll get a complete rundown on exactly how to calculate effects of almost any variation you may encounter, and how to adjust your play so you can be a consistent winner against virtually any Blackjack game under almost any conditions.

Now that you're sure of the rules of the game as it is played today, we'll take a look at how you can use them to your advantage. You're in for some pleasant surprises.

As you know, Blackjack is the only casino game you can beat

Go West, Young Man?

During Nevada's early gold and silver mining days, men packed up their horses and mules with picks, shovels, pans, grub and assorted paraphernalia to seek their fortune in Nevada's countryside.

Today, the opportunity has shifted to Nevada's glittering towns, and men need only bring the paraphernalia of information stored inside their heads to strike out in air-conditioned jets and taxis and have more potential for making a strike than most of those early miners had.

And, if nothing else, a heckuva lot more fun. . . .

Oddity

Blackjack is the only casino game at which an amateur can learn to consistently win. Yet, casino owners make more money off this one game than any other.

Why?

Because the armament most people bring when they buck the 21 tiger is insufficient to the job: chance, fortune, luck, speculation, fate, destiny, ESP, astrology, numerology, hot hunches and ineffectual systems just don't get it.

Stick with us. We'll show you how to really get it on.

consistently without luck. By mastering the Expert System, you will simply be using superior knowledge to beat the gamblers at a game for which they made up the rules!

So read on and discover how the Expert System can make you one of the few who can outsmart those slick gamblers who make millions each year from people who only *guess* at playing the game.

Genius, that power which dazzles mortal eyes,
Is oft but perseverance in disguise.

Henry Willard Austin

A reasonable probability is the only certainty.

E. W. Howe

Our doubts are traitors,
And make us lose the good we oft might win
By fearing to attempt.

Shakespeare

He will hew to the line of right,
let the chips fall where they may.

Roscoe Conkling

Those oft are stratagems which errors seem.

Alexander Pope

2 Expert Basic Strategy

Basic is Basic is
Basic is Basic

Hungry:	*Never mind footprints on the moon, science's biggest blast was inventing the computer. That perfected Basic Strategy and some fancier ways to eat up these hotshot owners at their own game.*
Mrs. Ms.:	*I thought sure you'd get food in there somewhere.*
Hungry:	*Well, no matter where I play Blackjack in the world, science made it possible to jet in live Maine lobster for my complimentary meals, but. . . .*
Grinder:	*The best thing about Basic Strategy is how easy it is; you just memorize a few things and wipe out the entire house percentage against you without even keeping track of cards.*
Party:	*Then you tack a few things onto it and the party's on. . . .*

About 20 years ago a group of scientists came up with an amazing bit of research: the common honeybee was incapable of flight. They even proved it; the wingspan of the bee was too short, the angle too shallow, the beat pattern too slow and the bee's body weight was too great.

About the same time, another group of scientists published a simple set of rules which gamblers could learn to very nearly nullify the house percentage at Blackjack. The scientists predicted it would be the end of Blackjack.

Despite all this scientific hocus-pocus, Blackjack games—and bees—have been flying just fine ever since.

To get you off the ground at beating Blackjack we'll forget the bee and concentrate on *how* that simple set of rules—called the "Basic Strategy"—which attempted to void the house advantage has evolved. The Basic Strategy originated more than 20 years ago. Since then, mathematicians and computer experts have refined it to a fine degree, and it is now a beautiful thing in action.

For Basic completely removes the guesswork from playing 21. You just sit back and play the hands without keeping track of cards or using any mental gymnastics. And you have complete confidence you have nullified the game to where it is almost dead even. *Almost.* For despite Grinder's optimistic statement that "you wipe out the entire house percentage against you," it is statistically inevitable that if you play $1,000 at $1 a time for 1,000 plays, you are absolutely mathematically bound to lose 15 cents against a single deck game using Las Vegas rules. Grinder just has to stop his wild exaggeration!

Now, here's a spot for most people to check—and improve—their game quickly. Take a look at the Basic Strategy charts and compare their recommended plays against your own. Some of the plays may look strange, but remember; if you are an average player *not* using Basic, those 1,000 plays we mentioned at $1 each would put you an estimated $60 to $160 behind rather than 15 cents. So you can see, using Basic faithfully is nothing less than dynamite!

Using our Basic is therefore vital to being a consistent winner at 21. It is the bedrock to anchor the powerful system you will shortly be given. And Basic to that system is like wings to the bee—you will fly even though no one thinks you can.

So how did the super-smart casino owners get sucked into offering a game at which they potentially had no edge and which some players could even beat?

They were really just lucky.

The first of the luck was that when they began offering 21 no one knew how to figure the odds. All the owners knew was that at the end of almost every day, when they added up profits, Blackjack was a big winner. After about 30 years of winning, no one really worried about figuring odds.

You Can't Win Them All

A few years ago, Grinder was playing in one of the Strip hotels when two elderly women dropped into the game, both sitting to his left.

On the next hand, Grinder was dealt 19 and stood. The first woman had a 10 and a 6. She looked at the large stack of chips in front of Grinder and said, "You seem to know how to play this game . . . what would you do with this hand?" He noted the dealer's upcard was a 7, and said, "Well, I'd hit it, myself."

The woman did, and drew a 5, for a safe 21.

The next woman doubled down with an Ace and a 5, a very poor play against an upcard 7.

The dealer flipped his hole card over, a 5, for a total of 12. He hit it with a 6, for a grand total of 18.

The woman who doubled caught a 10, for a "stiff" total of 16, and the dealer took her money. She turned angrily to Grinder. "Look what you did, Mr. Wiseacre. If you had told her to stand pat, I would have doubled down and caught that 5 and made 21, and the dealer would have caught that 10 and gone broke. That way we all could have won, instead of just you two!"

Unfortunately, the woman forgot she had a full drink in her glass when she gestured towards "you two," and the two winners each collected a generous splash of Tequilla Sunrise.

Moral #1: You could improve on the Basic Strategy a lot if you could play each hand twice.

Moral # 2: Don't give free advice unless you have a large cleaning budget.

Then the scientists stepped in about the early 1950's with some stringent mathematical analysis. The first to publish a serious technical critique were Baldwin, Cantey, Maisel and McDermott in 1956. The next year they published a popular book, *Playing Blackjack to Win*—and the first Basic. Then the blockbuster: Dr. Edward Thorp published *Beat the Dealer* in 1962. In addition to changing Basic slightly, Thorp revealed a card-counting system which he proved could consistently beat 21 against the rules then in effect. In his next edition, he published an improved system as a result of extensive computer runs handled by Julian Braun of IBM

Corporation. Thorp himself "proved" the system in live and much-publicized play against the casinos.

The owners panicked, changed the rules of the game, and almost undid themselves. Their customers, or "live ones," stayed away in droves while the real pros learned to adjust and went right on playing. Casino owners finally woke up and read their profit reports, and quickly changed the rules back.

And really got lucky.

For now there was enormous interest in Blackjack. And while it was theoretically possible to beat 21 using Thorp's system—the only one most folks had access to—not one in ten thousand was capable of using it! It was too complex, confusing, and for most people, virtually unworkable in action. But since it was *theoretically* possible to beat the game, customers flocked in and profits soared.

An interesting sidelight: when Thorp first published, Grinder and Hungry were furious. They had already been playing a winning system for several years and figured Thorp had killed the Golden Goose. As Hungry tells it today: "We were just turning big money with no one the wiser when this square blows the whistle on the whole thing. Whew! What could he possibly get paid for writing a book, $10,000, $20,000? We'd have given him that just to keep his mouth shut."

Now Hungry and Grinder laugh about it. "You know," Grinder says, "it turned out he did us an inestimable favor. When the outsiders flocked back in they brought more money than ever, and gambled it on systems too difficult for most people to play without an extensive math background. The average customer simply didn't understand that any system which is great in *theory,* but which is too demanding under actual playing conditions, is worse than no system at all."

Nothing has changed drastically since Thorp, except a dozen or so people have jumped on the system-selling bandwagon. Many of them attempt to "simplify" Thorp's original card-counting system, which is much like streamlining a dinosaur. No insult intended to Thorp's brilliant mathematical work—don't forget dinosaurs once ruled the earth. But conditions have changed, so even if you are capable of handling a ten-count system like his, it simply

---

The "Enormous" House Percentage

Take a look around Nevada and see the glittering hotels and casinos which cost tens of millions of dollars, and which generate hundreds of millions of dollars in profits annually. It's easy to see that profits from gambling are huge.

But it's stunning to realize that those profits are generated from relatively tiny, almost insignificant percentage figures. Consider:

On the pass line in craps, the house has a 1.4% advantage against players.

At roulette, the house usually has 5.26% against players.

At baccarat the house maintains 1.06% against the banker; 1.24% against the player.

From those tiny figures, fabulous casinos grow and thrive.

Blackjack is even juicier for casinos, depending upon how unknowledgeable its players are.

The average player has from 6% to 16%–or more–against him.

In this chapter alone, Blackjack Your Way to Riches tells you how to cut the house percentage against you at Blackjack to virtually 0%.

And wait until you see what's coming. . . .

---

can't deliver the profit of more modern techniques. And profit—with maximum undetectability and versatility—is where it's at.

Enough background for now. If you would like more detail on the fascinating saga of Blackjack research over the last 20-odd years, check the appendix for a list of intriguing reading, which includes the most significant works published. However, let me make a suggestion: *Don't get sidetracked or confused,* as much of what you will find is either outdated or out-of-touch with present playing conditions.

Let's review for a second the stages you are going through to become a consistent winner at 21. You've checked the rules; the next step is to memorize Basic Strategy to effectively neutralize the house percentage against you. After you've done this, you will learn the simple method of keeping track of cards developed by my contributors, and which will gain you incredible playing power. Since Basic is basic, let's get some basic questions out of the way.

What exactly is Basic Strategy?

It's the mathematically correct way to play any given hand off the top of the deck, and on average through the deck, against any dealer upcard, without considering any other cards played. Billions of hands have been played on computers to calculate the optimum Basic way to play hands without keeping track of cards. Expert Basic Strategy in this book incorporates the finest elements of 20 years' research—and includes a little of my own research and a lot of my contributors'.

Why doesn't everyone use it?

Two reasons: first, it takes a few hours to completely master it. (If *you* don't have that kind of time we'll present a simplified version which will give you a dynamic increase in playing power which you can learn in less than a half an hour.)

Second, most people who attempt it expect too much too soon; they are not looking towards the long run. After losing a hand or two, they decide Basic must not be very good and start innovating. This is a definite never-never! You must play correctly according to Basic to get its long range benefits. *Never* deviate at this point. And even after you are playing the Expert System, which does deviate at times, you will still play Basic about 80% of the time.

What's the house percentage and exactly how does Basic overcome it?

Blackjack is unique in that the house advantage is different against each player, depending upon his skill. In all cases, though, the entire house edge is based on the fact that you must draw and run the risk of breaking before the dealer; should you break, he takes your money even though he also breaks later.

For an exact advantage figure, however, let's say you play just like the dealer (hit 16 and under and stand on 17 or above, never double, never split, but still get the Blackjack bonus). The house edge is about 4.6% against you. Table 1 explains how you yank back that awful advantage (craps is only 1.4% against you with flat bets on the pass line).

Easy Aces: Figuring Hard and Soft Hands

Since the Ace can be counted as one or eleven, many players have trouble determining the hard and soft total of a hand that contains one or more Aces. Here's the way experienced gamblers do it.

If your hand contains one or more Aces, count each Ace as one to figure out your hard total. Then add 10 to the hard total and that will give you your soft total.

For example:

Your hand consists of Ace, 5, 2. Counting the Aces as one, your hard total is 8. Add 10 to this and your soft total is 18.

Your hand contains Ace, Ace, 2, 3. Counting each of the Aces as one, your hard total is 7. Add 10 to this and your soft total is 17.

You have a 10, 5, Ace, Ace. Your hard total is 17. Add 10 to this and your soft total is 27. Since 27 exceeds 21, you could only use the hard total of 17 in this example.

TABLE 1

Gain by Playing the Basic Strategy,
As Opposed to Playing Like Dealer

Approximately

Proper hitting and standing decisions	2.55%
Proper doubling down	1.55%
Proper pair splitting	.50%

Gain for player of about 4.6%

The numbers have been rounded, but you can see playing Basic effectively nullifies any house advantage. Remember, if you want this kind of gain, you must make correct playing decisions according to Basic Strategy all the time until you learn to keep track of cards.

As you saw, the biggest single gain in using Basic comes from using proper hitting and standing decisions. Keep in mind you are playing the total of your hand against the dealer's upcard. Table 2 is the hard hit-stand strategy in chart form.

TABLE 2

Hitting (Drawing) or Standing with Hard Totals

Your Hard Total	Dealer's Up Card									
	2	3	4	5	6	7	8	9	10	A
12			▒	▒	▒					
13	▒	▒	▒	▒	▒					
14	▒	▒	▒	▒	▒					
15	▒	▒	▒	▒	▒					
16	▒	▒	▒	▒	▒					
17–21	▒	▒	▒	▒	▒	▒	▒	▒	▒	▒

▒ Stand
☐ Hit

With hard 11 or less, you hit unless you are doubling down or splitting pairs.

Notice that all the dealer's possible upcards are shown across the top of the chart; all possible totals of cards you can have run down the left side. It works like a multiplication table—you go down with one and across with the other until they meet for your correct decision. For instance, if you have a total of 12 and the dealer's upcard is a 3, you hit.

You can see how easy this strategy is. Boiled down into a few words, the table tells you that if the dealer has a "good" card up (7, 8, 9, 10, or Ace), you hit 16 or less until you get 17 or more. If the dealer has a "bad" card up (2, 3, 4, 5, or 6), stand on 12 or more, the exception being to hit 12 against a 2 or a 3. Simple as it is, the hit-stand aspect of Basic is the single most important decision area.

Now, the hit-stand decisions for "soft" hands. A soft hand is any combination of cards which has one or more Aces and which cannot exceed 21—or go bust—with a single draw. For instance, Ace-2-4 (soft 17 with the Ace counted as 11) would not go bust if you drew a 10 count card. The hand would then become "hard" 17, (Ace-2-4-10) with the Ace counted as 1.

TABLE 3

Hitting or Standing with Soft Hands

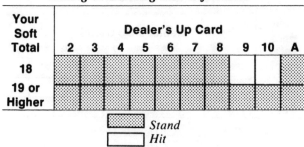

Your Soft Total	Dealer's Up Card									
	2	3	4	5	6	7	8	9	10	A
18	Stand	Stand	Stand	Stand	Stand	Stand	Stand	Hit	Hit	Stand
19 or Higher	Stand	Stand	Stand	Stand	Stand	Stand	Stand	Stand	Stand	Stand

Stand

Hit

Draw to (hit) soft 17 or less unless you are doubling down.

You may double down a two card soft 18 vs. a dealer upcard of 3, 4, 5 or 6. See table 5.

The rules for soft standing are really quite simple: you stand on soft totals of 18 or higher with this single exception—if the dealer shows a 9 or a 10 as an upcard, you stand on soft 19 or higher. In any case, you always draw to soft 17 or less unless you are doubling (described below).

It's important to note that tables 2 and 3 work together. Say you draw to a soft hand and it becomes hard; you then continue to play according to the "Hard Total" table. For example, say you have Ace-6 (soft 17) and the dealer has a 10 up. The "Soft Hands" table tells you to hit, so you do and receive an 8. You now have hard 15 (Ace-6-8) and you immediately play out the hand according to the "Hard Total" table—you hit again with 15 against a 10.

Double Trouble

Doubling strategy really spells trouble for the casinos, for when you add this to your hit-stand strategies you've cut the opposition's edge to (about) half a percent against you. Tables 4 and 5 tell all.

Notice you always double on hard 11. With hard 10 you always double, except when the dealer has a 10 or an Ace up. And you

TABLE 4
Hard Doubling Down

Your Hard Total	Dealer's Up Card									
	2	3	4	5	6	7	8	9	10	A
9	Double Down	Double Down	Double Down	Double Down	Double Down	Hit	Hit	Hit	Hit	Hit
10	Double Down	Double Down	Double Down	Double Down	Double Down	Double Down	Double Down	Double Down	Hit	Hit
11	Double Down	Double Down	Double Down	Double Down	Double Down	Double Down	Double Down	Double Down	Double Down	Hit

▓▓ *Double Down*
☐ *Hit*

Hit hard 8 or less unless you are splitting pairs.
Never double down on hard 12 or higher.

TABLE 5
Soft Doubling Down

Your Soft Hand	Dealer's Up Card				
	2	3	4	5	6
Ace-2	Hit	Hit	Hit	Double Down	Double Down
Ace-3	Hit	Hit	Double Down	Double Down	Double Down
Ace-4	Hit	Hit	Double Down	Double Down	Double Down
Ace-5	Hit	Hit	Double Down	Double Down	Double Down
Ace-6	Double Down	Double Down	Double Down	Double Down	Double Down
Ace-7	★	Double Down	Double Down	Double Down	Double Down

▓▓ *Double Down*
☐ *Hit*
★ *Stand with Ace-7 vs. 2.*

Never soft double vs. a dealer up card of 7, 8, 9, 10 or Ace.
For hit-stand decisions with soft hands, see table 3.

double with hard 9 only if the dealer's upcard is a 2, 3, 4, 5, or 6. Of course, you simply hit hard 9 if a given casino's rules prohibit doubling on that total.

Notice that anytime you have Ace-3, Ace-4, Ace-5, Ace-6 or Ace-7 you double against the dealer's 4, 5, or 6. Also, if you have Ace-6, you double against a dealer upcard of 2.

Naturally, if a casino prohibits soft doubling, you hit or stand according to table 3, "Hitting or Standing with Soft Hands".

Doing the Splits

Splitting is the least important of what you've had so far because you only get the opportunity to split approximately two percent of the time. So memorize this one last, but remember—every little bit you take away from them helps.

TABLE 6
Pair Splitting

Your Pair	Dealer's Up Card									
	2	3	4	5	6	7	8	9	10	A
2, 2		▓	▓	▓	▓	▓				
3, 3			▓	▓	▓	▓				
4, 4										
5, 5										
6, 6	▓	▓	▓	▓	▓					
7, 7	▓	▓	▓	▓	▓	▓				
8, 8	▓	▓	▓	▓	▓	▓	▓	▓	▓	▓
9, 9	▓	▓	▓	▓	▓		▓	▓		
10, 10										
A, A	▓	▓	▓	▓	▓	▓	▓	▓	▓	▓

▓ Split
☐ Do Not Split

Where you do not split, total the two card pair and refer to the hard hit–stand (table 2) or hard doubling down (table 4) charts.

Since this is least important, here's a modified splitting procedure to use until you're ready to tackle the exact decisions:

    ACES AND EIGHTS .... Always Split
    ALL.OTHER PAIRS .... Never Split

This is handy, but if you're serious about making money playing 21, master the entire splitting strategy after you have committed the other strategies to memory.

Decision-Making Sequence

Oddly, the order in which you make decisions in play and their order of importance to you in percentage gain are inversely proportional, that is, bass-ackwards. For in actual play, the decision-making sequence goes like this: first see if you have a pair and if you can possibly split it; then see if you can possibly double-down; then, if you can do neither, decide whether to hit or stand. But the order of importance in percentage gain to you runs the reverse: the most important is hit-stand decisions (2.5%); second is doubling (1.5%); and last is splitting (.5%). That's why you need to be on friendly terms with pair-splitting before you begin playing seriously. Decisions which get you the least gain are ones you have to consider first, and *can* have an effect on doubling and hit-stand.

Basic for Certain Unusual Conditions

If you should play in one of the rare casinos which allow you to double down after splitting, follow the pair-splitting procedure in table 7. By doing so, you will change the casino odds from very slightly against you to slightly in your favor.

No Hole Card

In some foreign casinos, the dealer might not take a hole card until after players have made their decisions. If you play in such a game, make the following modification in your strategy: do not double down with 11 versus a dealer's 10 or Ace. Also, do not split 8-8 versus a dealer upcard of 10 or Ace. You don't want to give him a chance at any extra money should he complete a Natural at his turn of play.

TABLE 7

Pair Splitting When
Doubling Down after Splits is Permitted

Your Pair	Dealer's Up Card									
	2	3	4	5	6	7	8	9	10	A
2, 2	▓	▓	▓	▓	▓	▓				
3, 3	▓	▓	▓	▓	▓	▓				
4, 4				▓						
5, 5										
6, 6	▓	▓	▓	▓	▓					
7, 7	▓	▓	▓	▓	▓	▓				
8, 8	▓	▓	▓	▓	▓	▓	▓	▓	▓	▓
9, 9	▓	▓	▓	▓	▓		▓	▓		
10, 10										
A, A	▓	▓	▓	▓	▓	▓	▓	▓	▓	▓

▓ Split
☐ Do Not Split

Where you do not split, total the two card pair and refer to the hard hit–stand (table 2) or hard doubling down (table 4) charts.

Surrender

Should you play in one of the casinos which offer Surrender, throw in your hand and take back half your bet anytime you hold 16 versus a dealer's 10 or Ace; and again, when you hold 15 versus a dealer's 10.

The Ultra, Super, Dynamite, Razzamatazz Refinements

You remember I told you that this book contained the techniques the real pros use, and that I would do my best to knock out the frills and garbage that comprise a large part of most Blackjack systems?

Well, I won't call your attention to it every time, but this is a spot you might be especially interested in.

Lose 15 Cents?

We made the statement that it's statistically inevitable that if you play $1,000 at $1 a hand, you are mathematically bound to lose 15 cents against a single deck game using Las Vegas rules.

Lose 15 cents while playing dollars, when the dealer either takes or pays you a buck?

It sounds like madness, but it's really just a way of expressing conveniently a mathematical expectation in money terms, rather than percentage figures (0.015%).

Actually, you would have to make 6,667 bets at $1 per hand before the house earned its first dollar ($6,667 × .00015 = $1.00).

What it all really means is that the house percentage against you is so negligable that you could be ahead or behind a couple of bucks after so many plays and no one could really be certain which way it would go.

It also means you don't need much more to tip the scales in your favor.

Right now, some authors are making a big to-do about some fancy Basic Strategy modifications which take into consideration whether you are playing against one deck, two decks, four decks, etc., etc.,

In other words, you might hit a given hand (Ace-7 vs Ace, for example) when playing against four decks, but stand with the same hand when playing against a single deck.

It all *sounds* great, and very "sophisticated."

But it's bunk and junk, if you agree with a very basic assumption I'm making: the objective is to get the most money with the least effort.

Now, all of the highly-touted changes, which tax your memory with details which really aren't significant, don't give a return that could be measured in peanuts. Why not spend the energy on the good stuff where you'll measure the return in elephants?

And that information is what you'll find in the next chapter, on the Expert Count.

However, if you're among the insatiably curious, and would like

---

A Feel For Blackjack and Basic Strategy

You will get 12, 13, 14, 15, 16 and 17 as the total of the two cards you are initially dealt about 40% of the time. You will lose more often than you will win with these hands (including 17).

You will get a Natural, or Blackjack, once in about every 20 hands.

You will split once about every 80 hands.

You will double down once about every 10 hands.

The dealer will break about 25% of the time.

If you could have a total of 18 every hand, and the dealer played normally, you would lose all your money in the long run; the dealer's average hand is a little better than 18. That's why Basic calls for you to hit a little more than newcomers might think wise.

Wait'll you see how easy it is to determine when you can expect to have a better hand than the dealer. And how easy it is to take advantage of that knowledge.

Fun for sure, and that's in the next chapter.

---

a detailed explanation about all of this, you'll find a thorough discussion in appendix A.

Aids in Learning

First study the tables until you feel you know them pretty well, then grab a deck of cards and play yourself through random decisions. Have someone deal to you, or be both dealer and player. Refer to the tables when in doubt. Work up to playing a half dozen hands at once, making decisions quickly and without reference to the tables. It quickly gets easier and easier.

The only drawback to working out by playing is that doubling and splitting decisions come infrequently, just as they do in a casino, and many other decisions may not appear in a given play.

To force those decisions out, try the following: take a pair you wish to concentrate on (two 9's, for instance) and place them in front of you. That's your hand. Then go through the rest of the deck card by card as if each were the dealer's upcard. Call out the decision as each "new" upcard comes off the deck. You can then do the same thing with any other pair, or soft doubles or—for that matter—any troublesome hand.

Simplified Basic Strategy

I promised you a simplified system for Basic you can learn in less than half an hour. Learn these six things and you will knock the house edge down to less than one percent:

- Stand on hard 17 or higher .. vs ... Dealer upcard of 7, (Hit 16 or less.)   8, 9, 10, Ace.
- Stand on hard 12 or higher .. vs ... Dealer upcard of 2, (Hit 11 or less.)   3, 4, 5, 6.
- Stand on soft 18 or higher ... vs ... All dealer upcards. (Hit soft 17 or less.)
- Double down on hard 11 .... vs ... All dealer upcards.
- Double down on hard 10 .... vs ... All dealer upcards (Don't double anything *but*   except 10 or Ace. these hard 10 and 11 situations.)
- Split Aces and Eights .... vs ... All dealer upcards. (Never split any other pairs.)

Remember, though, while taking the short time to memorize this simplified version might be a giant step forward, it's not the best you can do. So, if you intend putting a nice-sized dent in the gamblers' bankrolls by moving on to the Expert Count System, you *must* be very familiar with the entire Basic.

Avoid Psych-Out

Again, please remember that although Basic works out virtually even in the long run, it is also the best possible way to play in the short run as well, when you're not keeping track of cards. If you've played Blackjack, you know whichever way you decide to go with, say, 16 against an upcard 7, you are in a very bad position. But with Basic, for every 100 times you hold that particular hand and have $1 bet, you will gain $10 by hitting. It's still an overall losing hand, but instead of having a mathematical expectation of losing about $48, you only lose $38 per 100 hands of 16 vs 7.

That's why you don't get psyched into guessing. And you don't

---

Blackjack Your Way Past TV Commercials

One of the pleasantest ways to learn the Basic Strategy is to pick up a decision or two every time a commercial jumps onto the tube. This can not only be productive, it can keep your brain from turning to jelly. Or soapsuds. Or otherwise going snap, crackle and pop.

Dealers for Hire, Free . . .

Since using the Basic Strategy holds Blackjack to virtually an even gamble in the long run, you need only master Basic to effectively thereafter have dealers "work" for you for free while you iron out the rest of the Expert System. That price for labor is nice, and no university or trade school in the country can match it!

Doing it Under Fire

You have a total of 14 against the dealer's upcard of 10. The player next to you asks you for a light, and then for an ashtray which is on your left. The cocktail girl touches your arm and says, "Did you order the Harvey Wallbanger?" Off to your right a bell goes off and you notice a slot player has just won $5,200 for three quarters wagered. The dealer asks for your decision. What is it?

---

listen to gamblers, dealers, or pit bosses who base their advice for playing on last night's winners or losers.

Remember that 20-odd years of research we talked about that went into developing Basic Strategy? You don't have to delve into all of it for convincing proof of how Basic came about, but if you'd like a strong mathematical explanation of many of the Basic plays, grab a copy of Thorp's *Beat the Dealer*. Don't get lost; you don't have to understand how

$$E(t_0) = 2P(t_0 > \tau) + 2P(\tau > 21) + P(t_0 = \tau) - 1$$

works to be a tough player. Save some energy for the simple count system in the next chapter which will make you a consistent winner.

Mechanics of Basic

Here's a mathematical explanation of some of the ways you squeeze more profit out of hands by using the Basic Strategy.

Win More by Enhancing Winners

An example of this is when you hold hard 11 versus a dealer's upcard 6.

If you do not double down, but instead draw one card (which will give you 12 or more, and at which point you stand), you will

Win 61% of hands

Tie 8% of hands

Lose 31% of hands

for a net win of 30% of money bet. However, if you double down, your profit on the 30% net winners will be twice as much as it would be if you did not double. (At $1 per hand for 100 hands, you will win $30 by drawing and $60 by doubling.)

Win More By Cutting Losers

An example of this is when you hold Ace and 6 versus dealers 7.

When the dealer has a 7 up, he will make the following totals for every hundred hands:

37 times he will make 17	*(37% of time)*
37 times he will make 18–21	*(37% of time)*
26 times he will bust	*(26% of time)*

(Continued)

A Final Word

You've now learned how to use Basic to reduce the odds against you to about even. Be aware, though, that rule variations, as well as use of multiple decks, cause odds against you to fluctuate, depending upon the exact casino you play against. It's not always negative; sometimes the Basic player will have an actual advantage, other times a disadvantage. As you read on, you'll discover the exact effects of rule variations, how they affect you and precisely what to do about it.

Granted, you'll expend some effort in the learning process. If it seems difficult at first, don't become discouraged; your win potential can be enormous. Have confidence, and Grinder, Hungry, Party, Mrs. Ms. and I will make sure you have all the information

---

Mechanics of Basic (Cont.)

But if you draw to soft 17 versus the dealer's 7, you will gain an additional 15 hands per 100 hands when this situation occurs.

So, by standing you lose 37% of the time. And by drawing, you lose only 22% of the time. You gain 15 hands, or 15%, by drawing over standing.

Another example of winning more by cutting losers is the case where you hold a 10 and a 6 versus the dealer's upcard 7.

If you stand, you lose 48.3% of hands.

If you draw, you lose 37.7% of hands.

Therefore, you decrease your losers with this hand by 10.6%.

Win More by Reversing Losers

An example of this is when you hold two 8's versus the dealer's upcard 7. If you draw to 8-8, you have a

> 27% chance to win
> 6% chance to tie
> 67% chance to lose

for a net loss of 40%.

But if you split 8-8, you have almost a 10% net win expectation on each hand for a 20% total net win expectation.

Therefore, you have changed a 40% net loser into a net winner of almost 20%, a swing of 60% by playing the hand according to Basic Strategy.

---

you might need to be as good at playing Blackjack as you want to be. That's a promise as solid as the fact that bees can fly.

So first things first. You're off the ground when you learn Basic Strategy (you don't need to know it perfectly before going on). And you'll shortly be buzzing into the winner's circle with the Expert Count in the next chapter.

So fly.

Believe one who has proved it.
Believe an expert.

Virgil

They laugh that win.

Shakespeare

Shallow men believe in luck.

Ralph Waldo Emerson

Luck is infatuated with the efficient.

Persian Proverb

3 The Expert Count

Count yourself into
the winner's circle

Mrs. Ms.: *As far back as I can remember, Daddy (Grinder) always had black ($100) chips stacked on the dresser, and alongside them, reams of paper covered with mathematical formulas. Meanwhile, I flunked math in high school. Then, when I was old enough, and disillusioned with the kind of pay women make, I asked him to show me his card-counting system, knowing I'd never be able to do it. Just the counting part took five minutes to learn and in two hours I could keep up with him.*

Party: *That count is something else. I don't understand the formulas either. Who cares, as long as it works?*

Grinder: *Who cares! You two are inflicted with ingratitude— you're riding in a Rolls Royce on wheels Hungry and I invented. Sure, you've bought some computer time, but the real work was getting the program together. Do you know how many hours I. . . .*

Hungry: *Don't let them pull your leg. It's easy to be loose about it now that there's a jillion winning hours on the system, especially for those two, who never missed a meal. But back when we were doing the heavy refining—after Thorp got everyone excited looking for counters— it wasn't so easy.*

Grinder: *It was a bit grim. There we were, inventing formulas for favorability, playing efficiency and optimum strategies, all in the middle of assuming the clubs would be changing rules every other day.*

In just two hours from now you can add so much strength to your Blackjack playing power that you'll be able to prove conclusively that you can be a consistent winner at the game. In fact, by absorbing the information in this chapter and adding it to Basic Strategy, you will henceforth win most of the time. And your occasional losses should be comparatively small.

What that means effectively, is that by applying yourself now you can soon be a winner most of the time in the long run at actual casino play . . . and with only a few hours' work.

A strong promise, indeed, but very possible; for you are about to learn the most powerful and practical card-counting system ever to hit the popular market, bar none. From here on out, the casinos should never be ahead of you for long.

First, let's take a quick overview of the stages you are going through designed to take you to any degree of playing power you wish. You know Basic is basic and that you are adding techniques to gain muscle in the shortest possible time. In this chapter you will learn how to quickly be a consistent winner against single deck games using Las Vegas and Reno-Lake Tahoe rules (most Nevada single deck games use one of these) and against double deck games, using strictly Las Vegas rules.

The plan is to have you capable of making money quickly against these games, while you add the refinements which will enable you to go against almost any Blackjack game using almost any set of rules.

There's more to come, but why not earn while you learn, and get some extra experience to boot?

The step you're about to take is almost laughably simple— you're going to learn the Expert Count, that fabulous system my contributors developed for keeping track of cards. And you might know the *real* pros wouldn't work any harder at keeping track than they had to.

So why keep track at all? Well, while Basic Strategy holds Blackjack to virtually an even-odds game, the odds are definitely not even all the time. Twenty-One is unique among casino games in that the odds constantly change. Using Basic, at the *beginning* of a new deal, the odds are about even. Depending upon which cards come out, odds on the next hand from the same deck will

The Best Watering Hole of Them All

There is no place in the world with as much to offer the vacationer as Las Vegas, the ultimate oasis. You can only talk about it in superlatives: the best, the most, the greatest. I wouldn't kid you; I've logged more than a million jet miles thinking I would find a place with more to offer. It isn't there.

Vegas has entertainment unparalleled in all the world. The biggest, most spectacular shows, the now names lined up by the dozen and waiting to entertain you.

Even identical shows are better: the Lido in Paris is a shabby production compared to the way it's staged here.

The rooms, the pools, the facilities are the lushest, the cleanest and the best here. Almost everything we have in accommodations is new, brand new or recently remodelled. It's almost a fetish with us-everything must sparkle.

The pseudo-intellectual cum snob says we're garish, outlandish, spend millions on bad taste. They are unhappy unless they see a century or so of musty patina around them-and we're new!

The food is the most diverse, better prepared, plentiful and-for what you get-inexpensive.

Recreation abounds around us. In about an hour from here you can either snow ski or water ski. Sights, like Red Rock Canyon, Boulder Dam, Lake Mead, Mt. Charleston. Hunting, hiking, camping, fishing.

The sun beats down on us year 'round. Too blasted hot in the summer, but you can jump in the pool or hit the air conditioning the instant you feel the need.

Our lights make Times Square and Picadilly Circus seem like candles flickering in a hurricane.

We are Oz, and they are snooze.

I'm partisan and biased because I have been to the other places and usually found them outstanding in, perhaps, only one or two features: scenery, or food, or recreation, or. . . . But Vegas has it all.

Maybe some people wouldn't want to live here . . . because the desert is unusual and most exciting when it's a change of pace. And we don't have all the cultural advantages we should have. And we have the usual urban problems.

But to vacation, and to live for a moment in a fantasy of light and color and entertainment and with the very best of everything, Vegas is the ultimate oasis.

either be better for you, worse, or the same. As cards are taken out of play, the remainder of the deck can hold some pretty wild swings in percentage for or against you. And the odds keep changing as cards are played until the dealer shuffles all the cards and starts a "new" deck with the odds about even again. But mathematically speaking, about ⅓ of the time the odds favor the house, ⅓ of the time the odds are about even and about ⅓ of the time, the odds actually favor you.

The trick is knowing which ⅓ is which, and that's an important part of a count system—favorability measure. And when you know that, you bet as much money as is practical (see chapters 4 and 6) when you have the edge, and let the dealer deal to your minimum bet when the odds are even, or the house has the advantage.

While all valid count systems measure favorability, all published ones to date are generally either so simplistic (only keep track of 5's or Aces, etc.) they overlook many juicy betting situations, or so complex and brain-busting that you can't use them in actual play (quick, divide 14 by 17, if the ratio is more than .8, then you . . .).

Don't hit the panic button; the system you are about to learn doesn't require memorizing cards, computing ratios or using indices. You will use it easily in actual play and it will automatically analyze who has the advantage and to what degree as hands are played. Duck soup.

So what exactly is the system measuring? Though it requires some pretty sophisticated math to understand how you can get accuracy down to the thinness of a bee's wing, the general principles are easy:

When the deck contains a higher proportion than normal of high cards (9, 10, Aces), you have a definite advantage.

In general, here's why:

. . . With an excess of high cards remaining in the deck, your chance of getting a Blackjack increases. True, the dealer has the same chance, but you get paid 3 to 2 and he only gets even money.

. . . With an excess of high cards the dealer will break more often, since he *must* draw to 16 or less. Therefore, you can stand pat more and let him break; you can soft double and split pairs more with a better chance of success.

A Bunch of the Boys (and one Ms.) Were Whooping It Up

A couple of martinis, good friends, a couple more martinis. During dinner, good conversation turns to challenge: "I'd bet if we gave you the top system of all time, two things would happen. One, you couldn't sit still long enough to write it all down. Two, no one would believe it."

No more martinis for a year. A lot of interviews, tapes, conversations, details, data, sweat, computer runs. My end accomplished.

And you can Blackjack your way to riches.

. . . With an excess of high cards remaining, you have a greater chance for a good hand when you hard double.

Now the bad news.

When the deck contains a higher proportion than normal of low cards (2 through 8) the house has a definite advantage.

In general, here's why:

. . . You get fewer Blackjacks.

. . . The dealer breaks less often, and you therefore have less going for you when you soft-double and split pairs.

. . . You don't make as many good hands when you hard double.

. . . You generally have less going for you because you hit and break before the dealer and lose whether he breaks or not.

With this general understanding of how deck composition affects the odds for or against players, you can see the advantage of learning a system which precisely measures those odds.

Of course, measuring favorability is only one job a system has to do well to be great, and there have been many systems devised which attempt to achieve greatness by taking into account various aspects of the game. These systems range from poor to excellent in specific areas: simple or complex to use, plain or fancy depending upon the parameters they measure, and powerful or puny, depending upon how accurate their accompanying strategy is.

But for power, efficiency and yield in actual play, the system you're about to read beats all *practical* systems at any price.

Blackjack Pioneers

There are a number of top flight professional players who have made significant contributions to Blackjack system play and card counting concepts. For obvious reasons, these unheralded pros must herein remain anonymous.

Following is a rundown on those pioneers who have chosen, for one reason or another, to divulge generally the concepts that they have discovered, researched and are aware of.

Baldwin, Cantey, Maisel, McDermott. *Credited with computing (on hand calculators, yet) and publishing the first essentially correct Basic Strategy, back in the early 1950's.*

Edward Oakley Thorp. *Without doubt, Dr. Thorp is the man most responsible for the development and publishing of Blackjack strategies. Thorp's original computer program was the forerunner of popular Blackjack counting techniques used today. Though published in the early 1960's, his book,* Beat the Dealer *is still an excellent, if somewhat complicated, study on Blackjack.*

(Continued)

Practical is stressed for an important reason. Theoretically, you could get the maximum possible gain from a system based on hauling an IBM computer into a casino, feeding it information as the deck depletes, and having it tell you exactly what to do in a given instance. That's not only impractical, it's just about impossible and would probably result in you and/or the computer being barred.

Too, the advantage of using a computer in play would be that it handles complex things endlessly without fatigue. And now I must confess. There is one system for about $200 available which supposedly has a yield close to the Expert System. Unfortunately, it is so complex only a computer—and a few math wizards—can play it. Not surprisingly, the people I know who bought it and are capable of playing it, are severely limited in the amount of time they can play without falling victim to fatigue, and related errors.

Unfortunately, people are fascinated by complexity, and often make the mistake of assuming that a system which is more com-

---

Blackjack Pioneers (Cont.)

Thorp published the first accurate strategies for determining favorability and for playing hands when using a counting technique. His "Ultimate Count" was the forerunner of many point count techniques still used today.

Lawrence Revere. *Revere undoubtedly did more to introduce the average player to the concept of playing winning Blackjack than any other previous writer. A successful popularizer, Revere was also responsible for developing various point count subsets, simplifying the point count value in relation to the number of cards remaining, and attempting to make Blackjack system play easier to understand.*

Revere's book, Playing Blackjack as a Business, *published in the middle 1960's, provides an excellent historical perspective on many of the earlier Blackjack strategies.*

Julian Braun. *Noted for developing the most sophisticated and accurate computer programs of his time for the computation of Blackjack strategies. His computations were used by both Thorp and Revere in their books.*

---

plex must also be more powerful. That's why you find system pushers who are able to hustle one system for single decks, another for two decks, another for four decks and so on . . . and all systems complex enough to convince the befuddled buyer he is getting something good for his money.

On the other end of the scale are the very simple systems for sale. Many of these will win if you hang in there long enough; they just don't win very much or very often.

Alas, the systems jungle is populated with an incredible diversity of critters between "simple" and "complex," and all of them have varying ranges in cost and credibility. For instance, one popular book advises you to learn different—and somewhat outdated—systems which are presented almost one each per chapter. That book climaxes by offering some very expensive systems— which are presumably better—to players smart enough to buy something *not* outdated. That's like offering a cattleman oats which have been cycled through the horse once before giving him the opportunity to buy the fresh oats he wanted in the first place.

Another system offered in the mail for about $100 has the unfortunate distinction of being expensive, complex and having an extraordinarily low yield. Yet another book is very simple, fairly expensive, but doesn't work at all.

Fortunately, in the gamut of systems there are even a few which are reasonably priced and deliver a fairly decent win rate. If you're interested in detailed analysis of all popular systems, and an exposé on system peddlers, see chapter 7 for information on how to get our *Special Report on Blackjack Systems*.

I like to think of the Expert System you've purchased in this book as the new King of Blackjack techniques. The fact that the Master System described in chapter 7 is superior doesn't change my thinking—the Master System is not designed for the popular market and is intended for only a very few serious players.

To give you an idea just how powerful the Expert System you've bought is, consider the specifications I wrote down when I began considering this writing venture. No matter how much I knew about it, or what my experience was, I did not wish to put out "just another" Blackjack system. If my contributors' system did not meet these criteria, I would not consider writing about it:

1. The system had to be reasonably simple. While complex systems excite mathematicians, applying some of these impractical brainchilds in actual play can be laughable. Surprisingly, the complexity of a system does not make it more powerful. In fact, what many complex systems attempt in one direction, severely limits them in other areas because of their inflexibility.

2. The system had to be easy to learn. Who needs a system you have to dedicate your life to master?

3. It had to be uncomplicated to use in actual play. There are many distractions in gambling casinos and any good system should not require too much energy to use amidst occasional noise and confusion.

4. It had to be versatile. It's ridiculous to suggest a player learn one system for single decks, another for shoes, etc. A good system should have the capability of being used under all conditions effectively.

Comparative Shoppers Welcome

The Expert System isn't the only system designed for the popular market, it just happens to be the best.

In case you already have–or are considering purchasing– another Blackjack system, please turn to chapter 7 and read about our offer of a Special Report on Blackjack Systems.

This Special Report compares and analyses all of the popular systems on the market and rates them as to Betting Efficiency, Playing Efficiency and Practicality. One reading can save you hundreds, perhaps thousands, of dollars should you decide to play 21 in earnest.

In the Special Report you'll find informal writing which gets right to the point, and enough sophisticated math and data to satisfy the most exacting mathematician. It's all there, so you can make up your own mind.

The Special Report on Blackjack Systems *puts the search- light of truth on the hucstering and hullabaloo of most of those high-powered system hustlers.*

We welcome comparison.

---

5. *It had to win in actual use at a rate at least as good as any workable system on the market at any price!* After all, the name of the game is winning money. All the real pros want to know is, will it get the money and how long will it take? If my contributors didn't have something which would get more faster, what was the point of publishing at all?

6. *It had to be up-to-the-minute in taking into account casino conditions today, and flexible enough to adjust should conditions change tomorrow.* What could be more obvious than that?

7. *It had to be playable relatively fatigue-free.* Fatigue results in errors which result in losses. Also, the longer you can play without tiring, the more you can win.

8. *It had to be of the "Point" count type, wherein values are assigned to each card.* Counting actual cards (such as the number of tens remaining) is now obsolete. The advent of multiple decks and the policy of not dealing down to the bottom of the deck make

---

Bookstore Review: **Gambler's Book Club**

This is the place! At 630 South 11th St., Las Vegas, NV 89106, you'll find the largest collection of books on gambling anywhere in the world. Individual games, magic, horse racing, fact, fiction . . . anything you have an interest in concerning gambling is right here under one roof.

If you need help on any gambling subject, you'll find an outstanding staff of straight-shooters who will guide–but never hustle–you. Browse for an hour or a day, there's much more available on gambling than you ever imagined. And more to come, for the Gambler's Book Club is reprinting rare and out-of-print gambling books, as well as printing new books regularly.

If you can't make it there, send for a catalog. No, we have no business association and they didn't print this book. We wanted you to know you're in Luck, man, when you find good people to do business with.

---

non-point counting techniques as bizarre as trying to keep up with freeway traffic in a horse and buggy.

9. *The system had to count the Ace as a neutral card and not as a high card.* For years most mathematicians and uninformed authors decreed counting the Ace as a high card (gave it a minus point value). The *real* pros knew this was absurd, but were not about to wise-up any outsiders. Although the Ace behaves as a high card for betting, it acts as a small card for decisions which affect the play of the hand. Pros simply count the Ace as a side card and do not include it in the count. That clearly increases the overall effectiveness of the Expert System. Further, there is a simple way to adjust for Aces when betting.

10. *The system had to prove itself early, with the potential of adding on more power and sophistication as you progress.* What good is going through the drudgery of memorizing gobs of things *before* you even know if a system works? Better to be a winner early, then add power as you want to see your stacks of chips grow higher and faster.

Publisher Review: **Rouge et Noir, Inc.**

This outfit does good work. Its newsletter, Rouge et Noir News, is packed with valuable information monthly: Blackjack news, worldwide playing conditions, lawsuits against casinos, book reviews, gambling conference papers, junkets, etc., etc., and much more. This newsletter is carefully researched and quite accurate. You need it to keep current, and that it will keep you. You can also get back issues, valuable for background.

No, it's not a love affair and we have no business association.

Rouge et Noir also offers a book, Winning at Casino Gaming. It covers all types of casino games, and has some fascinating insights into such phenomena as superstition, luck and extra sensory perception.

Write P.O. Box 6, Glen Head, NY 11545 and get on their mailing list. You'll want to subscribe to the newsletter as soon as you start playing Blackjack for profit.

This last is the exact stage you've arrived at—you're about to tack just one more skill onto Basic Strategy and become a consistent winner. But let me tell you how amazed I was at my own—and the computer's—analysis of the total system.

IT MET OR EXCEEDED ALL MY IMPOSSIBLE EXPECTATIONS!

And I don't say that lightly. For in my time, I have thoroughly mastered the five most powerful systems published today, and played and won with all of them. (I mentioned before that some systems *do* work with varying yields.) But the Expert System proved itself better than any or all of them!

So let me state again: there is positively no other system which is both simpler and more powerful than the Expert System (the Master System is a bit more powerful, but a bit more complex). I'll be glad to prove this claim mathematically or in actual play to anyone who will make it worth my time. Any self-styled authority who disputes this claim would be well-advised to read our *Special Report on Blackjack Systems* before challenging.

Now for the Expert Count itself, that incredibly powerful method of keeping track of cards which is the cornerstone of the Expert System.

The Expert Count separates the deck into high, low and neutral cards, and assigns a positive, negative or zero value to each group. This enables you to continuously measure the difference between the key high and low cards. The cards are assigned a value as follows:

Card Denomination	Expert Count Value
King	−1
Queen	−1
Jack	−1
10	−1
9	−1
Ace	0
2	0
8	0
3	+1
4	+1
5	+1
6	+1
7	+1

You start at zero and keep a Running Count, or cumulative total, as each card is exposed during play. When you see a high card (9, 10, Jack, Queen, King) you subtract one point from your total. When you see a low card (3, 4, 5, 6, 7) you add one point to your total. A neutral card (2, 8, Ace) does not change your total. Since there are an equal number of high and low cards in the deck, your count starts at zero and ends at zero.

For example, assume the following cards were exposed: 3, 7, Ace, 5, 6, 10, King—in that order. By starting your count at zero, your cumulative total would run: 3 (+1), 7 (+2), Ace (is neutral, so the count would still be +2), 5 (+3), 6 (+4), 10 (+3), King (+2).

In Joke

When Party first started playing, he had this happen:

A woman rushed up to the table and counted out $87.50, which she placed in a betting square. "I dreamed I was absolutely going to win this hand," she said, and pulled her coat around to try and conceal the nightgown she wore underneath.

She drew two tens and the dealer had a six up.

"I knew it!" she said, and showed the hand to Party.

The dealer promptly hit and made 21.

The women stormed out of the casino towards the hotel elevators, taking her two cards with her.

The dealer, amused, watched her leave, scooped up her bet, then asked Party what her hand was.

"Minus two," he replied.

When your cumulative total, which we'll call the Running Count, is positive you have the advantage. If your Running Count is negative, or minus, the house has the advantage. If you have a zero Running Count, odds are about even.

Generally, the higher the plus total at the end of each round of play, the more advantage you have going for you and the more you should bet on the next hand from the same deck. When you have a negative or zero total, make a minimum bet. Of course, you play the hands according to Basic Strategy.

And that does it! By using the Expert Count, betting more when you have an advantage, and playing Basic Strategy for the decisions, you will be a consistent winner in the long run against single deck games using Las Vegas or Reno-Lake Tahoe rules, and against double deck games using strictly Las Vegas rules.

But before you take these skills into a casino, DO NOT UNDER ANY CIRCUMSTANCES GO OUT AND PLAY UNTIL YOU HAVE READ CHAPTER 4 on "Money Management" AND CHAPTER 6 on "Keeping Your Name on the Welcome Mat." Now that you are capable of being a consistent winner at 21, you need to know how to keep casino personnel from detecting you, and how to protect your money.

You are, however, now in a position to test this part of the system in your home.

First you might find a proven method of learning how to count useful.

Easy Steps to Count Mastery

1. Take a deck of playing cards, turn one card over at a time and call out the count value, $+1$, -1, or 0. Do this until you instantly recognize the *Expert Count* value of each card.

2. Go through the deck one card at a time and keep a Running Count, adding or subtracting each card from the previous total as it is exposed. The count starts at 0 and ends with 0.

If you haven't used negative numbers in a continuous operation like this, table 8 should be very useful.

TABLE 8

Positive and Negative Numbers

Numbers get larger in this direction

$\rightarrow \rightarrow \rightarrow \rightarrow \rightarrow$

etc. $-9 -8 -7 -6 -5 -4 -3 -2 -1\ 0 +1 +2 +3 +4 +5 +6 +7 +8 +9$ etc.

$\leftarrow \leftarrow \leftarrow \leftarrow \leftarrow$

Numbers get smaller in this direction

An easy way to gain quick familarity with using positive and negative numbers is to use your finger as a pointer with the above table. Start with your finger at 0. With your other hand turn over cards from a full deck. As a plus $(+)$ card is revealed, move your finger one notch to the right. As a minus $(-)$ card is revealed, move your finger one notch to the left.

For example, say the first card you turn over is a 3, that's a plus 1 so you move your finger one notch from 0 to the $+1$. The next card is -1 and you move your finger to the left, putting it back at 0. Say the next card is also -1; you move your finger again to the left and you have a Running Count of -1. Say the next card is another -1; you move your finger to the left again and the Running Count is

---

Pretty Please-Challenge Us-Pretty Please

My contributors and I have often observed that most Blackjack system sellers challenge each other to games to prove something or other-usually, who can get the most publicity.

My contributors and I agree we will gladly accept all challenges under the following conditions:

Any game must be for a minimum of $500,000.

No publicity must accompany any contest which has as a prize an amount from $500,000 to $2,000,000. Those low prices are simply not worth losing our anonymity for.

Any game for more than $2,000,000 can have all the publicity any challenger can arrange. Only one of my contributors or I will accept, however, as that is retirement pay suitable enough for only one of us.

The minimum amounts stated are to be the sums realized on a net basis, that is, after taxes.

The game arranged should be a freeze-out under mutually acceptable rules and conditions.

Any game for under $2,000,000 should be arranged for by writing the publisher, who will contact us directly. Do not publish any challenge before contacting us directly. We would consider that an attempt to get free publicity.

All figures stated herein should be adjusted upward annually to account for inflation.

−2. Now say you get a +1 card, you move your finger to the right and the Running Count is −1, etc.

3. Now go through the deck turning over two cards at a time. Total each set. For example, you turn a five and a ten, the total is zero. Don't attempt to keep a Running Count yet, simply practice until you instantly know two card totals.

4. Run through the deck turning two cards over at a time and keep a Running Count. After you get good at this, keep a Running Count as you turn over both one-card and two-card combinations.

5. Have a friend deal 21 to you. Practice keeping the count and playing each hand with Basic Strategy. When you can start and end the count with 0, you're ready for your home test of this winning strategy.

Card-Counting Procedure in Play

Whether at home or in a casino, stick to this procedure for counting cards during play. We'll do face-down games first.

Count the value of the dealer's upcard first ($+1$, -1 or 0), then add or subtract the total count value of your two cards. Next, plug in all the values of all cards drawn by other players as they are exposed. If a player goes bust, add in his hand as it is exposed. When the dealer draws to his hand, count each card value as it hits the table. Finally, when the dealer is settling bets, add any remaining cards which were not exposed previously. This way, you are keeping a Running Count with all exposed cards accounted for in a logical order.

In face-up games, proceed a little differently. First count all other player's *two-card* combinations, starting at the dealer's left and proceeding as he deals the second card to each player. Of course, you keep a Running Count. Then you count the dealer's upcard; then count each card drawn by players. Finally, count the dealer's hole card as he exposes it, and any hits taken by him.

Betting: The Ideal Bet Size

For now, and only for the home test of this system, you will bet in direct proportion to your advantage: the higher the plus, the more you bet. The best way to do this is to bet a number of chips equal to your Running Count when it is plus: at $+1$ you bet one chip, at $+2$ you bet two chips, at $+3$ you bet three chips, at $+4$ you bet four chips.

This is your Ideal Bet Size, but never bet more than four chips no matter how high the count gets: at $+8$ you still bet four chips. Naturally, at zero or any minus count, only bet one chip. You make all decisions according to Basic Strategy.

This is exactly how you would like to bet in casinos as well, but again, DO NOT PLAY IN CASINOS UNTIL YOU HAVE READ *CHAPTERS 4* and *6*. Among other factors, while this betting technique will enable you to test the system at home, increasing your bets too rapidly in a casino is likely to alert personnel you might be counting.

So why test the system one way and play it another in action? This enables you to test the system while gaining skill in using it,

---

Missing Cards During Count

If you occasionally miss counting a card during play, ignore it except to make a mental note that your count may be slightly off. However, if at all possible, try and figure what the card might have been. If you can't, consider the card random and it shouldn't affect your overall return in the slightest.

Here's an example of figuring out what a card might have been that you missed:

The player to your right hits and receives a 10. He busts and throws in his hole cards and you only see one of them, another 10. You could probably assume the other card was a 2, 3, 4, 5, or 6. That's because most players don't hit 17–21, so the unseen card probably wasn't a 7, 8, 9, 10 or Ace.

Since the odds are greater that the unseen card was either a 3, 4, 5, or 6 (rather than a 2), your count would not change, as a 10 with a 3, 4, 5, or 6 is equal to zero.

Thus, you can often estimate cards you miss fairly accurately. And although you should strive to count perfectly at all times, occasional random errors in counting–as long as they aren't biased–will have almost no effect on your overall return.

---

and it cuts down testing time. Also, this is *approximately* how you will bet in action. And last, any betting system also requires thought, and you will likely need all your wattage for playing Basic, keeping a Running Count and using this simplified system of bet variation for now.

Examples

It's really much easier actually playing with cards than looking at examples in print. Nonetheless, I'll talk you part way through a single deck to demonstrate the sequence of events as you play. It's a lot easier in practice than it looks here, though.

We'll assume you're playing head-up (alone) with the dealer, the deck has been shuffled, and the hands go like so:

First hand. Bet one unit. Dealer upcard: 7. Running Count: + 1. Your two cards: Q, 6. Running Count: still + 1. Your Basic Strategy decision: hit with 16 vs. a 7. Hit card: 4. Running Count: now + 2. You stand. Dealer hole card: 5. Running Count: now + 3.

Dealer hit: 7. Running Count: now +4. You win the hand, with 20 vs dealer's 19. You win one unit.

Second hand. Bet four units at +4. Dealer upcard: 10. Running Count: goes to +3. Your two cards: Ace and 7. Running Count: now +4. Your Basic decision: hit. Your hit card: 5. Running Count: now +5. Your decision: hit again with 13 vs 10. Your hit card: 7. Running Count: +6. Dealer's hole card: 8. Running Count: still +6. You win with 20 vs dealer's 18, and collect four units.

Third hand. Bet four units (your maximum bet) at +6. Dealer upcard: 3. Running Count: goes to +7. Your two cards: 9-3. Basic decision: hit. Your hit card: 10. Running Count: goes to +6. You broke, dealer turns over hole card, an 8. Running Count: still +6. You lose four units.

Fourth hand. You bet another four units at +6. Dealer upcard: 9. Running Count: now +5. Your two cards: Ace, 9. Running Count: +4. You stand. Dealer's hole card: 10. Running Count: +3. You win with 20 vs 19, and collect four units.

Fifth hand. You bet three units at +3. Dealer upcard: Jack. Running Count: +2. Your two cards: 10, King. Running Count: 0. You stand. Dealer's hole card: 9. Running Count: −1. You win three units.

Sixth hand. You bet one unit at −1.

And so it goes, though much more quickly than it took you to read it.

As you test the system, make sure you give it a long enough trial to be absolutely convinced it will work for you in the long run. Somewhere between 100 and 500 hands should convince you for sure.

If you're a crackerjack at Basic and counting already, an even quicker test of the system is possible. Take four plus cards out of the deck entirely (one 3, one 4, one 5, one 6), start your count at +4, bet the same way and your count should end at zero after you've gone through the deck.

What you'll be doing is giving yourself more favorable betting situations, situations you would have to wait for in live play, but which would eventually occur anyway. Between 50 and 250 hands of this should leave you holding all the chips.

Where to Sit

Usually, try to sit anywhere from the center of the table to the last seat on the dealer's right (third base). The idea is to sit where you can see as many cards as possible without being obvious. This is especially helpful when you get into "Advanced Expert Techniques."

A good thing to remember is that third base is where counters are traditionally expected to sit.

These are general guidelines; when you really get good, any seat is great.

Slowing the Game Down

After you've played Blackjack awhile, your biggest problem is speeding the game up without appearing obvious. Your Expert System lends itself to rapid play, and when you know what you're going to do with every hand it doesn't take much time to do it. Most people hem and haw a bit more than occasionally, and that looks the most natural.

However, when you're just beginning, sometimes you need a moment or two for a decision. Anytime you do, remember this ironclad rule: the dealer cannot go past you until you have clearly indicated your decision.

So take the time when you need it. Everyone understands when someone has a legitimate decision to mull. They also have come to understand that a player may be attempting to count cards if he, say, ponders too long with what to do with a Black- jack. Or what to do with a pat 19 vs an upcard 6. In that kind of case, it might look as if he is either very new to the game or trying to count.

When you can keep an accurate Running Count using the Expert System card values, can play Basic perfectly without looking at the tables, and are convinced the system works, go directly to chapters 4 and 6 ("Expert Money Management" and "Keeping Your Name on the Welcome Mat"). You're just about ready to knock 'em in the creek.

He hath indeed better bettered expectation.

Shakespeare

True luck consists not in holding the best cards at the table:
Luckiest he who knows just when to rise and go home.

John Hay

Lack of money is the root of all evil.

George Bernard Shaw

A fool and his money are soon parted.

16th Century Saying

Expert Money Management

Everything you need to know to
handle units, dollars, marks,
francs, pesos, pounds, rand, yen,
won, guilders, schillings, dinar,
bolivar, krona, drachmas, lira,
escudos, piastres, etc., etc., etc.

Author: *What do you figure you made on that last trip to the French Riviera?*

Hungry: *About $12,000.*

Author: *Before or after expenses?*

Hungry: *After, of course.*

Author: *Did you pay for your own transportation that time?*

Hungry: *Yes. I felt like playing and didn't want to wait for the junket. Cost me about $1500, first class.*

Author: *So you made more than the $12,000?*

Hungry: *Of course. You wouldn't count expenses in the win figure, would you?*

Author: *Did you buy any souvenirs?*

Hungry: *Well, yes. I bought an antique chest for $2,000. That would make my win figure higher, I guess, but I thought you wanted to know how much cash profit I came back with. . . .*

Author: *Buy any clothes?*

Hungry: *For crying out loud, you have to have something to wear . . . about $800, but. . . .*

Author: *Entertainment?*

Hungry: *Okay, okay. A few shows, maybe a couple of meals the clubs didn't pick up, maybe three nights on the town and a day or two on the stopover in London. . . .*

Author: *How much a day do you figure you spent?*
Hungry: *Oh, say, three or four hundred a day, if you count my
lady friend.*
Author: *All this not counted in the $12,000 win figure?*
Hungry: *How can you count it in? A guy has to eat, has to have
clothes, has to go where the money is, has to have
companionship and knick-knacks.*
Author: *Let's see. That comes to about $6,000 or so more than
the $12,000 figure, or about a real win of $18,000?*
Hungry: *You don't understand. When I leave I count my money;
when I get back I count it again. The difference is what I
win or lose, right?*
Author: *How long did you actually play to make the $18,000?*
Hungry: *About 23 or 24 hours spread over six nights. Had a
pretty good betting spread, 50 to 5,000 francs. Got
stuck $3,500 at one point, then got back out with the
$12,000 . . . or $18,000 . . . or whatever you said. Oh, I
forgot to mention the watch I bought in Nice. . . .*

Imagine being an accountant and trying to make sense of Hungry's bookkeeping system. Impossible! And for a new player to use Hungry's system without equal skill and experience, disastrous.

Understanding all phases of money management is crucial to success at Blackjack. In fact, with proper management you will actually increase your playing power by winning at a steadier rate and more often, and conversely, by losing less and losing less often. Paradoxically, if you manage improperly you can lose money even though you are winning consistently! That's a mind-boggler, but definitely true. You'll see why as you read on.

So please read this chapter carefully before you put your money in action. Blackjack play often has many odd quirks which can be terribly hard on money if you're not prepared.

The Easiest One First

The easiest money problem to handle is the one most often overlooked, as did Hungry earlier: keep separate track of ex-

---

Getting the Clap

Whenever a dealer leaves a table he will usually lightly clap his hands together, then briefly expose his palms upward.
Do not take this as a brief burst of applause for your play. Most establishments require this ritual to be certain the dealer is not leaving the table with any chips.

---

penses and playing money. About the time you pay for two meals, a cab, give your wife $20 for the slots, and play Blackjack at a table or two all out of the same pocket, you're hopelessly in the dark as to what you won or lost. Especially when you use that method for a few days. When you know you can make $12,000 or $18,000—or whatever that was—everytime you go against them, do it Hungry's way.

The Hardest One Second

The toughest question to answer specifically is the one you probably want answered the most: how much money can *you* make playing Blackjack, given your particular circumstances. I obviously can't analyze your situation, but I will try and supply enough guidelines so you can make a knowledgeable guess.

What makes it tough to figure is that your win rate depends on a myriad of variables. Most Blackjack books juggle those variables and end up promising—or implying—an earning rate totally unrealistic in terms of the system promoted and/or the playing conditions of today. Unlike other books, this one won't duck the question by telling you stories about a few people who got rich quick, or tales of how some lucky cat won $50,000 in a weekend.

On the other hand, I will not back out on the claim that this book has the potential of earning you $100,000 or more a year. I'll tell you how to get that, if you want it, and also what you can expect to earn in less than full-time play.

Variables

So, exactly what are the variables you must dial into your calculation on what you can expect to earn? Here's a rundown

with some general comments; details on the more difficult ones
will follow.

Chip denomination. What you suspected is true—if you bet
$100 chips you will win much more than if you bet $1 chips . . .
about 100 times more.

Betting spread. If you could bet $1 when you have no advantage and all the way up to $10,000 when you have way the best of it,
you could own the entire state of Nevada in about a month.

Bankroll. You must have adequate funds to back your play.
You rarely, if ever, have a 100% win proposition. Therefore, if you
had a $100 bankroll it would be foolhardy to put it all on your first
bet.

How well you count. You must be able to count quickly and
accurately.

How well you play. If you can play just what you've learned so
far in this book 100% accurately, your earning rate will be higher
than if you partially learn all the material and play it 75%
accurately. That's why we set this up for you to add on stages of
power as you can handle them.

Mistakes. Everyone makes them. If yours are occasional, minor, and random, they will have little overall effect. If they are
major mistakes—such as reversing a count from, say, a minus 7 to
a plus 7—and making a maximum bet when you should be making a
minimum bet, you will likely lose more money than if you hadn't
read the book.

Freshness. If you give it your sharpest hours, you're less likely
to make mistakes than if you play after work or after a long trip.

Experience. When you have it, nothing distracts you from
playing properly. Say you're in the middle of a hand and you have a
big bet out. From nowhere a famous movie star appears, asks you
if the dealer is hot or cold, offers you a drink and bets $1,000 on
every open betting square. In front of you 14 pit bosses appear to
ingratiate themselves, and behind you one person for each dollar
wagered on the layout crowds in to watch. If you don't forget the
count and make the right decision, *that's* experience.

Rules. If you've learned everything presented so far, you only
lack money management techniques in order to consistently beat

Records and Record Keeping

You'll undoubtedly find that keeping records of all your plays will be very helpful, especially at first.

Records can be simple or elaborate, depending upon your memory and needs. The simplest meaningful record should include: Date, Shift or Time, Playing Time, Casino, Single or Multiple Decks, Win or Loss, Cumulative Win or Loss and Cumulative Time.

From these records, you should be able to compute your hourly rate of return, before and after taxes.

See appendix for some printed forms to start you out.

The IRS

We most emphatically call your attention to the fact that you must declare all your winnings (minus your losses) on your Federal income taxes, and whatever state tax forms which apply.

At least as persuasive as the fact that the law calls for it, is this analysis by Grinder:

"It's a basic mistake not to pay taxes. How can you spend the money if you don't? If you end up squirreling away the money in tin cans in your back yard, you're giving up chances for investments which will ultimately make you more money than the taxes took. Besides, you're taking a chance of being jailed or fined. It's definitely not worth it."

single and double-deck games against Las Vegas rules, and single-deck games against Reno-Lake Tahoe rules. There are still plenty of these games almost everywhere in Nevada and in some parts of the world, so you can now be winning while you gain experience. When you master the rest of this book you will be able to beat almost all games against almost any rules.

Shuffle point. You win at a greater rate the farther down in the deck they continue to deal cards. Right now, most places deal down to about half a single deck, a few to ¾ of a deck, and fewer still, all the way

Power of system. You'll win more with this system than with any other practical one in the world today, with the single exception of the Master Count mentioned in the last chapter. When you

---

Tipping

Tips, or "tokes" (for token of appreciation) are a welcomed–and too often, expected–supplement to dealers' incomes. After you've played a few days, you'll run across most of the nicest and nastiest ways various dealers hustle tokes. Be advised that most dealers want–and feel entitled to–all they can get. Many become abrasive when they don't get what they think they have coming. Some guidelines might be in order.

Don't toke at all until you know what your long-term hourly win rate is. Then decide how much you're willing to tip for services rendered.

Set up your own standards for tipping, much as you already do with a waitress in a restaurant. If a dealer is courteous, polite, reasonably smooth and is generally professional, that's worth something. If a dealer is peremptory and abusive, that's not.

How well you get your Expert System on might be a factor, but don't expect or act like a dealer is in collusion with you.

Dollar players should rarely, if ever tip . . . their win rate is not very high and there's not much advantage.

Players who bet $25 and higher can hardly escape tipping . . . they will be accorded too many privileges not to reciprocate a bit.

Never toke less than a dollar under any circumstances.

It's not a good idea to tip more than you're earning per hour, no matter how much you win at a given session.

Never toke when you're losing, unless there's an advantage in doing so.

(Continued)

---

nail down all details of the Expert System in this book you can even win with flat bets in many games! (A flat bet means betting the same dollar amount every hand with no variation in betting.)

Number of hands. You get a dealer who gives you 50 hands an hour and you'll win less than one who deals out 150 hands an hour (about three times less).

Proximity. If you live close to gambling, you'll be able to play and win more than if you only occasionally visit. More hours in, more money out.

Familiarity. If you play too long and too strong and win too much in too short a time and go to the same place too often, odds

> ### *Tipping* (Cont.)
>
> *If you're quitting winners, try to toke an amount which will insure your not being remembered as being too cheap or too generous. Experience will fill in the details.*
>
> *Tipping abroad runs the gamut from casinos which don't allow tipping to casinos which don't pay their dealers a salary, and thereby force them to depend on tips for income. Ask.*
>
> *The mechanics of tipping are easy. You can either push a chip or two over to the dealer when you've won a good hand, or are about to leave the table, or you can bet for the dealer.*
>
> *The last is best. That way the dealer wants you to win the hand, as he will win also.*
>
> *You let the dealer know you're betting for him by placing his bet a little forward of your own. If you get a double down or a split, you can make an additional bet for him if you choose.*
>
> *If you win, and you have bet for the dealer, he also wins and now gets twice the amount you would have given had you simply made a gift of the bet. If you lose, the dealer is kindly disposed towards you and looks forward to the next time you might bet for him.*
>
> *Most books recommend that if you're going to tip you only do so when the deck is plus and you want the next hand dealt. From the dealer's point of view, he hopes you "know" something when you make a bet for him. Don't be so obvious as to let him know that you do.*

are someone is going to begin associating your appearance with the money's disappearance. There are many ways around this (see chapter 6), but if you stick around to be watched closely, you'll have to make plays to throw the watchers off, and that will reduce your earning rate.

Juggling. All these factors can be juggled to get the same or different results at will. For instance, you may play Blackjack only once a year for high stakes and make more money than someone who plays year 'round for smaller stakes. Or, if you're extremely cagey in your play, you might be able to get a betting spread of from 1 to 10 by making calculated wrong plays at the right time and thus make more than if you bet carefully with a 1 to 3 spread in a larger dollar amount. Don't get anxious; details follow.

First Times Out

Until you have casino experience, the first time or two you go out, play strictly for practice using the smallest possible stakes. You've developed confidence maintaining the Expert Count and playing Basic Strategy at home; now you need to know you can do as well in a casino under much more distracting conditions: a different, perhaps faster, pace of play; other players who are talkative or morose; dealers who are surly or gregarious; plus other casino oddities, like cocktail girls who interrupt concentration by asking if you'd like a drink, lounge groups who play your least-favorite song, slot machines clanking and ringing, etc.

How Much Can You Afford to Win?

The question isn't as silly as it sounds. Before you can answer it in light of present playing conditions, you must take into account two problems sticky as a spilled pot of honey.

The first problem centers around this fact: the biggest single characteristic casino personnel look for, when trying to determine if someone is counting, is a sudden and drastic increase in the size of bets. They're suspicious of this, and if the big increase *always* comes after a bunch of little cards comes out, they will begin to take countermeasures. Granted, you're doing nothing illegal, but the operators don't like getting beaten at one of their own games and will try to protect themselves (see chapter 6).

Avoiding detection is therefore an important consideration when you're figuring how much you can afford to win.

The *reason* sudden big bets is a tipoff is simple. All valid card counting systems somehow measure big cards against little cards as they come out in play in order to determine advantage. The fact that the Expert System is superior for a variety of reasons is beside the point; the principle is the same. Now, you recall that when more little cards than big come out on one hand, the deck becomes plus and you have an advantage because there is a higher proportion of big cards remaining in the deck to be dealt on succeeding hands. Also, the higher the plus (meaning more little cards out and

---

Those Who Promise the Half Truth and Nothing But...

In all the books about Blackjack, not one has presented all the facts about money management you see in this chapter: earn rate named, variables isolated, what you can do and what you can't. Now that it's all laid out, you can guess what will happen:

"You can make a million dollars a year with. . . ."

"Now, twice the win-rate of the Expert System with half the effort. . . ."

"Proof the Expert System is 250% less accurate than. . . ."

For shame, for shame.

As you might suspect, all you have to do to make wild claims about earn rate is to ignore some of the variables involved in actual play, base figures on a bigger betting spread, assume everyone is oblivious that Blackjack can be beaten, etc.

If you really want to know what performance you can expect from any of the popular systems on the màrket, and have them compared to the Expert System, send for our Special Report on Blackjack Systems *described in chapter 7.*

It's going to make some faces red.

---

more big cards in), the greater the advantage. Therefore, it would seem to make sense to bet more every time your advantage increased.

Remember, in your home test of the system you did bet exactly that way, called "betting in proportion to your advantage," or your "Ideal Bet Size." At a Running Count of +3 you bet three units; at a Running Count of +4 you bet four units; and at a count of +1, zero or any minus you bet only one unit. You no doubt noticed that at times you would jump from a one unit bet all the way to four units (the suggested maximum we set). If you did that in casino play, some dealers might shuffle the cards—even though they suspected nothing—just to be safe. By shuffling and starting a new deal, no one has the advantage.

SPY

So in order to have the biggest bet possible out when you have the appropriate edge, and in a way to minimize the problem of suspicion, learn the betting modification my contributors developed to keep casino personnel oblivious. They call it SPY, for *Sly Proportional Yields*.

Until you gain experience, you are limiting your betting spread to a minimum of one unit to a maximum of four units (this four-unit spread means $1 to $4, $5 to $20, $25 to $100, 10 francs to 40 francs, 50 to 200 marks, etc.). You *attempt* to bet according to your Running Count, so that at +1, zero, or any minus number you only bet one unit. At +2 you can bet two units; at +3, three units; at +4, four units.

But never increase your bet more than two units over your last bet, no matter how favorable the count. In other words, if your last bet was one unit when the count was zero, your next bet would only be two or three units, even if the count jumped to +4.

Even after you have experience, it's a good idea to follow the above rule when playing against double deck games until the first full deck is gone, and only one deck remains to be dealt.

At the point there is only one deck left, SPY can really go to work for you to increase your advantage, assuming a little experience and discretion on your part.

Generally, you still maintain a 1 to 4 betting spread, increasing your bets by one or two units when the count calls for it. However, when the count is +4 or higher, and if you are winning, you can start increasing your maximum bet up to six units. That's easy, as you simply drop part of your payoff after a win onto your bet before the next hand.

This kind of betting looks natural as many people let all or part of any winnings "ride" on the next hand. But if you start losing after you've expanded your betting spread to six units, immediately go back to a four unit maximum bet at plus 4, and don't exceed four units no matter how high the count gets until you begin winning again.

Up to this point, SPY essentially has you betting within proportional limits, increasing your bets by one or two units when the count justifies it, and expanding your maximum bet when you're winning. All that is very safe and sound: you're not moving your money much and you should make steady gains.

But the real objective of SPY is not to follow any rigid betting

---

A Very Safe, Simple and Sound Betting Plan

If you want a simpler betting procedure which is very deceptive against single and double decks, consider this:

Bet one chip more than your last bet anytime your count is plus 2 or higher, to a maximum of five units.

You will not make quite as much money, your bankroll will fluctuate a little more, but you can hardly make it easier on yourself in making a betting plan work for you.

Cagey Losing

Most amateurs figure they can be a little more reckless in their play when they are losing. That's partially true; casino personnel don't pay nearly the attention to losers as they do winners.

But they definitely pay attention. And those foolish folk who put down a 1 to 10 betting spread when they're losing often find that they can't get down a 1 to 2 betting spread when they're winning. Reason: they've already obviously tipped their play.

---

procedure that could eventually be predictable. As you gain more and more experience, you'll begin adding subtle techniques which will make your betting virtually undetectable.

For instance, you can experiment with betting out of proportion to your advantage, for example betting four units at + 3 (if it looks natural) and if you are winning.

You might also bet a unit or two more on the minus side if you're winning a number of successive hands there. This would then entitle you to bet a little more on the plus side than your normal maximum, if you're winning. But beware of moving money on the minus side too much, as you will lose on the minus side in the long run.

Essentially then, SPY is a non-rigid proportional betting technique by which you bet more on plus counts (on balance) and less on minus counts (on balance), and in a way which casino personnel don't equate with counting, and in a manner which holds down capital fluctuation so you indeed get Sly Proportional *Yields* (you don't get *too* carried away with your maximum bets in relation to your minumum bets).

Thus, the SPY concept is limited only by your own ingenuity and cleverness at keeping casino personnel oblivious and loving your action as you win.

One caution, however. Do not misconstrue any of this to mean you should ride a "hot streak" for all it is worth on the minus side, or back off should you lose a few bets at plus counts. You must have more money out there (on balance) when the deck is plus than you do when it is minus or you are going to lose for sure in the long run.

Some general comments

Keep an eye on the deck and try not to have a large bet out at the point the dealer usually shuffles. If he does shuffle, don't be afraid to pull your bet back down to one unit, but don't do this too often with any one dealer. Remember, even if you *leave* your big bet out, the odds are about even.

If you run into a dealer who shuffles any time your maximum bet is out, odds are good he suspects nothing, but is being overly cautious (to impress the boss). Lower your maximum bet or find another table.

Since any betting system requires thought, it is a good idea to practice at home, if at all possible, before trying it in action.

Do a little experimenting with betting in actual play to see just how closely you can bet in proportion to your advantage without attracting attention.

Capital Requirements

Now that you've overcome the problem of jumping bets too suddenly, the second part of how much money you can afford to win concerns the amount of risk capital—or bankroll—you are prepared to back your play with.

Remember the paradox mentioned earlier, that you can be a consistent winner at Blackjack and still lose money? The reason is simple. No matter how good you get at the Expert System—or even if you should move up to the Master System—you will inevitably run into short, adverse runs of cards which will cause your capital to fluctuate downward (see Appendix). If your maximum bet is too large for your bankroll and you get caught in a bad

---

Rigid Flexibility?

That's what you need when you try to determine how long to play or how much money to win or lose at any one session.

For beginners, an hour is about right, or winning or losing a Session Bankroll.

But that's an approximation, not a steadfast rule. If you're winning every hand, shucks, go ahead and take the money or exceed the time. At the point the run stops, make one or two more bets and then leave on a losing bet.

Or suppose you sit down at an empty table and it fills up in five minutes, making conditions difficult. Find another table.

Or suppose you've been playing for an hour with two other people and they leave. You feel fresh, no one has noticed you, and you're about even. Stay a little longer.

Or suppose you've been there five minutes and you start feeling lousy. Leave.

The point is that you must play a great number of things by ear. You must be rigidly flexible. Don't lose too much at any one sitting, but don't limit your wins too much, either. Don't stay too long, but don't be so regular they can set their clocks by your comings and goings.

---

run of cards, you can be wiped out even though you are capable of winning in the *long run*.

For instance, it would not be wise to make just two $50 bets if you had a $100 bankroll. Nor would it be wise to put *all* of your money on any one hand if you knew you were going to win seven out of the next ten hands. In both cases, even if the odds were in your favor, just one or two losers would do you in.

Happily, bad runs are rather nicely balanced by equally sudden favorable runs of cards, during which you *win* far out of proportion to your advantage. But good runs pose no threat to your bankroll.

So remember, the house has almost an unlimited bankroll in comparison to any one player, and can therefore ride out *its* adverse runs. And you know, of course, that even though the house has a fat percentage against players of all games, it doesn't win *all the time*. If it did, no one would gamble.

The trick is to establish a bankroll size and a betting range which provides maximum safety to your money, and lets you maintain a steady win rate, while being able to absorb short, inevitable bum runs of cards.

Remember the long run. For in the short run, you might lose a few hands when your count is plus and you have the advantage, and win when the count is minus and you don't have the advantage. That means you're losing your big bets and winning the little ones during the short run, and you need to have enough capital to recoup and pull ahead when that adverse—and perhaps perverse—short run is over. After all, you don't win *every* hand when the count is plus, nor do you lose *every* hand when the deck is minus.

There's a psychological factor, also. If you over-bet your bankroll and lose a few critical hands it can affect your concentration and/or judgment and cause playing errors.

Of course, providing safety for your bankroll is vital so you know how much capital you must back yourself with to maintain the win rate you wish to achieve. Now that you're in position to appreciate the variables and factors that go into figuring an accurate win rate under present playing conditions, I think you'll be pleasantly surprised at what you can make.

We'll do the figuring in units so you can apply the figures to any denomination chip and to any currency anywhere. For instance, say a unit was $1. Two units would be $2; three units $3; etc. Or say a unit was $5. Then two units would be $10; three units $15; etc. Or say a unit was 20 Marks. Then two units would be 40 Marks; three units would be 60 Marks; etc.

Now let's pull together all the fragments we've been discussing into one formula. If it seems hairy at first, read through to the tables, which should help make it jell.

Win rate: Under present playing conditions, and using the complete playing strategy, you should win two maximum bets or more an hour. That means, if you're betting from 1 to 4 units using $5 chips, your maximum bet would be $20 and you should win twice that an hour, or $40.

Total bankroll required: It should be 30 times your top, or maximum, bet. That means, to provide reasonable safety against bad runs of cards, you should back yourself with $600 in order to

---

$$$ Additional Pointers $$$

You'll make more money in both the long and the short run if you:

• Play under the best conditions possible. *Single decks are better to play against than doubles. Head-up (alone) with the dealer is best–one or two other players at the table is okay, but a full table is slow and fatiguing.*

• Appear, and be, relaxed. *Don't look at cards obviously. Don't do anything to attract unnecessary attention, unless that's what you want. Don't play with money you can't afford to lose. Don't let distractions affect your concentration.*

• Learn the game completely. *Try to anticipate the dealer's shuffle point. Don't reach for your chips until you know what your next bet will be.*

• Take frequent breaks. *Be nice to yourself. Stay cool; you're not gambling.*

---

have a 1 to 4 unit betting spread using $5 chips. More conservative players might wish to have 40, 50 or even more top bets behind them for safety.

Session bankroll: This is an additional safety factor I haven't mentioned before. Never risk your Total Bankroll on any one playing session. Instead, divide your Total Bankroll into 5 equal Session Bankrolls. Then play until you have won or lost one Session Bankroll, or for one hour, whichever comes first. This is a good hedge against fatigue and related mistakes which can cause heavy losses, and against anyone getting too good a bead on your playing style.

If you ever lose two separate Session Bankrolls in a row, go back and review Basic Strategy and the Expert Count to see if you're making mistakes.

Betting spread: You choose it, to a suggested maximum of 1 to 4 units, based either on how much you wish to win or how much you have to risk.

The following table should be helpful. It has been calculated from units but converted into standard denomination chip amounts used in American casinos.

TABLE 9

Relationship of Betting Spread to Capital Requirements and Approximate Win Rate

Unit Size	Betting Spread	Total Bankroll Needed	5 Equal Playing Bankrolls (Each)	Win Rate (Per Hour)
$1	1–2 Units	$60	$12	$2 to $4
$1	1–3 Units	$90	$18	$3 to $6
$1	1–4 Units	$120	$24	$4 to $8
$1	1–5 Units	$150	$30	$5 to $10
$5	1–2 Units	$300	$60	$10 to $20
$5	1–3 Units	$450	$90	$15 to $30
$5	1–4 Units	$600	$120	$20 to $40
$5	1–5 Units	$750	$150	$25 to $50
$25	1–2 Units	$1,500	$300	$50 to $100
$25	1–3 Units	$2,250	$450	$75 to $150
$25	1–4 Units	$3,000	$600	$100 to $200
$25	1–5 Units	$3,750	$750	$125 to $250
$100	1–2 Units	$6,000	$1,200	$200 to $400
$100	1–3 Units	$9,000	$1,800	$300 to $600
$100	1–4 Units	$12,000	$2,400	$400 to $800
$100	1–5 Units	$15,000	$3,000	$500 to $1,000

Please remember this table is only an approximation of what you can win. Remember, all those variables are hidden in the figures and had to be accounted for on an educated-guess basis. However, be aware I am trying to be fair—many of those system pushers mentioned earlier make much more extravagant claims. In order to arrive at the figures given I relied on three things:

1. Computer data which measures system strength. This came out to figures with about a 25% *higher* return than the highest listed for win rate.

2. Extensive analysis of my contributors' records for the last year they played this system. They averaged about 20% higher returns.

3. A personal, 100-hour test of the Expert System in the places

where I was able to play without being recognized. My returns were about 10% higher.

Perspective

Now a few general comments to put the data into perspective. If you plan playing dollars it's difficult to get a lot of hands per hour as dollar tables get a lot of action and are often full. However, you can often get a bigger betting spread to compensate for this as dollar tables are watched less closely.

If you plan betting $100 chips, expect a lot of attention. After all, this makes you a high roller and management will be out to curry your favor. Also, figure to bet more carefully and less obviously and perhaps to cut down your playing time in order to allay suspicion. Your dollar win rate will still be very high, though you might not be able to maintain as high a unit-win rate after you start getting noticed.

So what you have are ball-park figures. As an obvious example of how they can fail, consider this: multiply the win-rate playing $100 chips with a 1 to 5 betting spread for eight hours a day times a 300 working-day year. You come up with a win figure of about $2,400,000. That amount would get Howard Hughes up to scrutinize the action. You'd never get it on.

Now, About That $100,000

Let's take a look at how to get that $100,000, or for that matter, any specific amount of money. Simply divide the number of hours you plan to play in a year into whatever figure you hope to reach, and the answer is how much an hour you have to make. Now check the table to see what unit size, betting spread and bankroll you need to employ and you have a reasonable approximation. Reasonable, that is, if you haven't overestimated your playing skill or underestimated conditions.

Some cautions, though. Most folks work approximately 40 hours a week and 50 weeks a year, or about 2,000 hours total. I would say that even if you lived here in Nevada, which has more Blackjack games than anywhere else in the world, it would not be possible to play 2,000 hours in a year for two reasons: 1) You would have to be extraordinary to maintain peak mental capacity for a full eight hours every day, and 2) You would probably begin to attract attention by just being around so much, especially if you played larger units. So, unless you are exceptional, figure your playing year at a more realistic maximum of about 1,000 or less hours, or something under four hours a day.

And here's a big caution. REMEMBER THE VARIABLES. If you can't play efficiently, or they are shuffling early, or you're not getting enough hands an hour, and so forth, all these will have an effect on hourly win rate.

I also can't stress enough the importance of *experience* before you play anything but dollars. Therefore, I strongly urge the following plan for moving up the chip scale in playing Blackjack.

Black is beautiful, but so is white

In order to win $100,000 or more a year you will probably need to play $25 or $100 chips. These latter are usually issued by most Nevada casinos in either black or white, but can be any color. Here's the best possible plan for progressing up the chip scale to $100 units:

Starting with 30 top bets for a betting spread of from $1 to $4, you need approximately $120 for a Total Bankroll.

When you have increased that amount to $600, play $5 chips *only* with a $5 to $20 spread. If you possibly can, start out with $5 chips, unless you need experience or are playing for fun. Dollar tables are usually crowded and difficult.

When you have increased your $600 to a minimum of $3,000 (or, to be safer, $4,000 or $5,000) you progress to $25 chips with a $25 to $100 spread.

When you increase your $25 chip bankroll to $12,000 ($15,000 to $20,000 would be safer), you may then begin playing chips with a $100 to $400 spread.

Time element

Starting with a $5 to $20 spread, under good conditions you should average $20 to $40 plus per hour, depending upon your playing ability and the casino conditions you encounter. If we assume you earn an average of $30 per hour, in 100 hours you should have your minimum $3,000 for a $25 chip bankroll.

Magazine Review: Gambling Times

Run by Stanley Sludikoff (né Stanley Roberts), this slick mag comes out of Los Angeles and contains timely articles on most phases of gambling, plus personality pieces, junket information, playing conditions world-wide, and much other information well worth the price. Write: SRS Enterprises, 839 North Highland Ave., Hollywood, CA 90038, for subscription information.

Playing a $25 to $100 spread, you should average $100 to $200 an hour. Assuming an average win rate of $150 per hour, you will probably win $12,000 in 80 hours of play. A $12,000 win plus $3,000 original bankroll equals your safer $15,000 bankroll for play with $100 chips.

Playing $100 to $400 spread, you should average $400 to $800 an hour. Assuming an average win rate of $600 per hour, you should win $60,000 every 100 hours of play, in the long run.

Since you are playing a minimum of approximately 100 hours at each level to earn enough money to proceed to the next level, you will have acquired a great deal of experience in play prior to progressing up the chip scale. That's very important.

General comments

Starting with dollars is impractical for serious players, though you should play dollars at first to gain experience and confidence.

Many people may not be able to progress to $25 or $100 chips because they feel too uncomfortable playing at those levels. Remember the fluctuation inevitable with any system. When that fluctuation occurs at the $100 level, you may temporarily be loser, say, $4,000. Even though you know that's only 40 *units*, and well within your bankroll safety margin, the experience can be very unsettling. Choose a level you're comfortable with and stick to it until you're really ready to move up.

You should never play at both the $5 level and the $25 level, or any such mix; play at one level only. If most of your plays are with $5 chips, and you occasionally decide to play $25 chips, one loss

---

If You'd Like to Play Against the Shoe Now . . .

There's much more precise information in chapter 5 for getting the most out of playing against four-deck shoes, or any multiple decks for that matter. But you can go ahead and beat multiples right now if you're satisfied with a formula without a lot of definition.

In order to know when you have the advantage, and when you can start increasing your bets against multiple decks, divide your Running Count by the number of decks you're playing against. If you come up with a count of +2 or higher after the division, you can then go ahead and bet with the same plan presented in this chapter. You still make your decisions according to Basic Strategy.

To clarify, if you're playing against a four-deck shoe, divide your Running Count by four. When one of those decks has been dealt, and three remain, then divide by three. When you get down to two decks, then divide by two. When you get down to only one remaining, it's the same thing as playing against a single deck. You always estimate to the nearest full deck.

You only need to do this division for betting when the count is plus, as at zero or any minus count you will be making your minimum bet. Examples:

Your Running Count is +4 and there are 3¾ decks remaining to be dealt from. You divide by four (estimate to the nearest full deck) and you get a count of +1. Since you don't begin increasing your bet until +2, you stick with one unit for the next hand.

The Running Count is +3. You wouldn't go to the trouble of

(Continued)

---

with the bigger units may cancel a large portion of your winnings at the $5 level. You can see that the loss of one *Session Bankroll* at the $25 level is the same as the loss of your *Total Bankroll* at the $5 level. This is another example of how poor money management can cause you to lose your money even though you are winning consistently!

So play consistently at one level until you decide to progress to the next level; then play consistently at that level.

Always pull the money out of one level to play at the next level.

If You'd Like to Play Against the Shoe Now . . . (Cont.)

dividing by either four, three or two decks, if you were playing against multiples, as it is apparent you could not end up with +2.

The Running Count is +14 and three decks remain. By dividing by three, you come up with a count of about +4 or +5. Go ahead and bet your maximum, our suggested four units at this point. That is, if it looks right (see SPY).

Right after you make the division to determine your bet size for the next hand, IMMEDIATELY GO BACK TO THE RUNNING COUNT. For example:

Your Running Count is +9 and you're playing against three remaining decks. You divide your Running Count by three and come up with a count of +3. You go ahead and bet three units on the next hand. THEN YOU IMMEDIATELY GO BACK TO YOUR RUNNING COUNT OF +9 in order to keep track of the cards.

The reason for this necessary division step is explained fully in chapter 5, "Advanced Expert Techniques." It really amounts to having to overcome a bigger house advantage when you play against multiple decks. Since overcoming this disadvantage takes more work, we still recommend you play against singles and doubles until you gain experience and confidence.

If those easier games are not available, and you wish to start making money as soon as possible, you can do it with this undetailed formula. However, this simplified version assumes the game you are playing against uses Las Vegas rules. If it doesn't, you might not be able to increase your bets until you have +3, or +4, or even more, after your division. And to understand how that all works, you'd probably better go ahead and read chapter 5.

Don't move up until you have made the previous level pay for it. Please understand that I, nor anyone else, can guarantee you can play Blackjack successfully, no matter how much information you have. Therefore, provide your own guarantee and peace of mind by moving carefully from level to level.

If You're Ready Now

If you already have the bankroll *and the experience,* and wish to immediately start playing for big money, I strongly urge you to

---

NO NO NO NO NO NO NO

We do not what we ought;
What we ought not, we do;
And lean upon the thought
That chance will bring us through.

Matthew Arnold

---

consider the Master System described in chapter 7. With that, you'll need less of a bankroll for a given betting spread, and you won't need as big a betting spread for the same win rate. In addition, the Master System is so powerful and tricky that you will sometimes make plays that would even mystify readers of this book. It should pay for itself at the level you'll be playing in less than an hour. It's quick and deadly, but I absolutely do not recommend it unless you already have extensive experience playing in the casino environment. The Expert System is definitely best for beginners (or most people for that matter), and given its simplicity, powerful beyond belief.

There's another reason I'm not recommending the Master System generally. My contributors are quite frankly a pain in the tail about it, and schizoid to boot. They are less than thrilled at letting it out at all and having other players around on a par with them. But since none of them are adverse to making extra money, they contrived the following conditions for selling the Master System: 1) They decide how many will be sold and to whom (system sellers need not apply), 2) They can withdraw from the offer of selling anytime they wish, no matter how *few* have been sold (they will limit the sale during any one calendar year should it appear too many people are interested in getting in on a good thing at their ultimate expense).

As for me, I have no reason to be less than candid: I have my job, I have my stash from a long time back, I have investments, I have this book, I have my own copy of the Master System—so why should I pull your leg? I repeat, do not consider buying the Master System until you have gained Blackjack experience and know that 21 is for you, and you want to take that big step up. Do something easy and powerful before you go on to something even slightly more difficult, however powerful.

A Final Word

That's about it for money management. You've arrived at the point where you are ready to be a consistent winner against single deck games using Las Vegas and Reno-Lake Tahoe rules, and double deck games using Las Vegas rules only. That is, if you can do these four things: keep an accurate count, play Basic Strategy correctly, vary bets properly, manage money carefully.

If at all possible, go out soon and play and prove to yourself you can beat these not so super-slick gamblers at one of their own games. Then read the next chapter on Advanced Techniques and tack on additional skills so you can win more faster and more often and against almost any Blackjack game with almost any rules. In fact, if you don't have the opportunity to get in action right away, go ahead and master all you can so you're even more skilled when you do go out. In either case, read chapter 6—"Keeping Your Name on the Welcome Mat."

You've now reached the point where I don't have to wish you luck . . . you don't need that, if you can handle the amazingly powerful Expert System. I do wish for you very soon to have that golden thought, that exciting moment when you suddenly realize, *it works . . . it's better than I thought . . . and it works for me!*

It is a bad plan that admits of no modification.

Publilius Syrus

Take calculated risks. That is quite different than being rash.

George S. Patton

5 Advanced Expert Techniques

Getting deadlier
with the Expert
System

Grinder: *You know, people aren't impressed by picking up a little here, a little there. They want you to promise something BIG, even if it's unrealistic.*

Party: *What do you mean?*

Grinder: *Well, you tell people they can add approximately one percent or so to their playing power by learning six things, and they would probably figure it isn't worth the trouble.*

Hungry: *Any increase in edge is great with me. And anytime I can make a couple more bucks just by memorizing a few things, that's worth the trouble.*

Mrs. Ms.: *There you go again, not being fair. Why don't you explain what a percent means in dollars instead of making it sound like a lot of trouble for not very much return?*

Grinder: *Well, it's fairly easy to estimate. Say you're betting $5 chips and your average bet works out to about $10. Now, with 100 hands per hour, you have about $1,000 in action, and a one percent gain would amount to an additional $10 an hour profit.*

Party: *Percentages bore me, but I'll tell you I didn't mind doing the homework when I found an extra one percent meant $50 an hour more than I was already making . . .*

> that is, betting quarter ($25) chips with a one to five
> spread.
>
> **Grinder:** Your return should actually be a little higher, shouldn't
> it, Party?
>
> **Party:** Yeah, but I do a little betting on the minus side to throw
> them off once in awhile.
>
> **Mrs. Ms.:** See? When you guys come down off those little per-
> centages and talk about $10 or $50 an hour increase,
> don't you think that makes it sound more like it's worth
> the trouble?

You are about to leave all other systems far, far behind, and increase your earning capability to a significant degree. In fact, when you've added these techniques, there will only be one other system in the entire world which is superior. That one, of course, is the Master System described in the last chapter, and not intended for popular sale.

What you will learn now does not merely boost your win-rate, though increasing returns is always a joy. In addition, the refinements make your Expert System superior in many ways.

Masking play

Instead of making the same play all the time according to Basic Strategy, as for instance hitting 15 against a 10, you will learn how and when the deck composition calls for standing with 15 against a 10. You will also learn to vary many other plays as well. And, you will learn when to take Insurance and when not to, and how to vary other aspects of your Blackjack play for greater return.

What all this means is that sometimes you execute a decision one way, sometimes another . . . and that makes it very difficult indeed to detect you as a card counter. A pit boss would have to know the Expert System as thoroughly as you in order to account for *all* your plays. And if he did, he would probably be out playing himself, rather than standing around in the pit.

In short, your play will not only be more lucrative and powerful when you know these Advanced Expert Techniques, but it will be more deceptive as well.

Making Mistakes

Take a look at your chest; if there isn't a big, red "S" on it, you're not Superman and you will make occasional mistakes. As long as they are random, and infrequent, it won't cost you too much. It's the big, consistent mistakes that put the large dents in your bankroll.

For instance, say you reverse a vital operation, like standing with stiffs (12, 13, 14, 15, 16) against 7, 8, 9, 10 and Aces. That will cost. But should you slip and only stand once during a play in one of those situations, your loss expectation is only a small percentage of your bet. You may win or lose the whole bet, but your expectation for overall loss doesn't become great until you make a number of mistakes.

Or, say you reverse a count from perhaps −5 to +5. The −5 meant you had a negative expectation of about 2½% and you should have been betting one unit. But instead, you thought you had a positive expectation and you made a big bet. It doesn't take much of that to make you a consistent loser.

To put the last case in mathematical perspective, look at it this way. At −5 with one $5 chip bet, your expectation of loss in 100 such plays is $12.50 (2½% × $5 × 100). If, instead, you reverse the minus to plus and bet $20 instead of $5, your loss expectation is $50.00 per 100 such plays. In other words, you will lose $37.50 more than you should have.

It really boils down to the "long run." Make a mistake once and it's anybody's guess what will happen—you may even win, and profit. But make it over a long period of time and the percentage against you will definitely come out.

Simplicity

You will be adding refinements to what you already know, and adding more power as you can handle it. Unlike other systems, you won't have to forget one thing and re-learn another in order to increase playing power.

Flexibility

As you add refinements you will be able to adapt the Expert System to play under almost all conditions: single deck, multiple decks, and against almost any rules, such as against casinos which don't permit doubling on anything or which don't permit splitting Aces (both cases are rare).

Mobility

With flexibility comes mobility. You'll know exactly how to play when you debark in London, the Caribbean, Germany, Spain, Cairo, or wherever 21 is played. You will know how to adapt the Expert System to play where you like.

In addition, you will see many other benefits as you progress through the refinements and incorporate them into your play.

THE SUPER SIX

The six most important elements of advanced play are:

1. Determining the "Exact Count."

2. Using the Exact Count to overcome rule variations and conditions.

3. Establishing a betting schedule, based on the Exact Count, by determining your advantage more accurately.

4. Modifying the Basic Strategy, based on the Exact Count.

5. Utilizing the Insurance bet, based on the Exact Count.

6. Adjusting the Exact Count as Aces are played.

You can see that the one common denominator to all six elements is the Exact Count, so we'll talk about that first.

What the Exact Count Is

First, let's review the Running Count for a second. Remember, you keep a Running Count by adding or subtracting the plus or minus value of cards as they are removed from the deck, as described in chapter 3.

The Running Count then tells you the numerical difference between the high and the low cards. For example, if your Running Count is +4, you know there are four more high cards remaining to be dealt from the deck than low cards.

Now, in order to determine what effect that numerical difference has on your advantage, you must relate that difference to the number of cards remaining.

For instance, if your Running Count is +4 and 52 cards remain,

---

Treat Your Body Good

If you're like most of us unfortunate mortals, you only have one body. It's a shame. For with a spare or two, you could get rich that much quicker.

Since you only have one, treat it well. Especially when playing Blackjack. The unexpected strain might surprise you, at first. To people outside your body it seems you are very casual, sitting and playing an apparently simple game.

But inside you a great deal is happening. Your mind races for a decision as you talk about the weather; you concentrate furiously as you off-handedly order a beverage from the cocktail girl; you are trying to gauge your next bet, when you suddenly notice you have not moved your left leg for half an hour and it has gone to sleep. . . .

All that and much, much more.

So remember to make short plays and take frequent breaks. Clear the cobwebs out. Jump in the pool. Take a sauna. Have a massage. Don't push too hard at any one session; the game will be there when you get back to it. Take a walk. Try deep breathing. Isometrics. Meditation. Eat well, but lightly, and heavy on the protein. And wear your galoshes when it rains.

In short, treat your body well and you will find that you will be sharper and more relaxed and you will win more. You work much fewer hours playing Blackjack than at most things, and earn more. But you want to be in top shape for every encounter.

However, feel free to keep a killing pace if you have a spare body. . . .

---

your advantage is approximately 2 percent. But if your Running Count is +4 and only 26 cards remain, your advantage is 4 percent. You have twice the advantage, though the Running Count remained the same!

So you see, you need a quick way to adjust the Running Count as cards are dealt in order to know your exact advantage. That's because the closer you get to the bottom of the deck, the greater the effect each point of the Running Count has on your advantage. To determine this effect precisely, you simply convert the Running Count to an Exact Count.

Single deck method

To make the conversion, you first estimate to within a quarter of a deck the number of cards remaining, and from which the next hand will be dealt. The easy way is to glance at the discard box; if there's approximately a quarter of a deck there, then about ¾ of the deck remains to be dealt; if half the deck is there, half remains. If the casino doesn't use discard boxes, you will have to estimate the upside-down cards on the bottom of the deck the dealer holds in his or her hand. Either way becomes easy with practice. Then use the following table to convert to the Exact Count.

TABLE 10

Converting Running Count to Exact
Count with Single Decks

Amount of Deck Remaining	Conversion Factor
1 deck	Multiply by 1 (same as Running Count)
¾ of a deck	Multiply by 1½
½ of a deck	Multiply by 2
¼ of a deck	Multiply by 4

Keep in mind that you are *estimating* to the nearest quarter of the deck, and that it isn't necessary to know *exactly* how many cards are gone.

You can see that for the first ¼ of a single deck the Running Count and the Exact Count are the same, since you multiply your Running Count by 1. But after the first ¼ has been dealt, the difference in proportion starts to be felt. Now, multiply your Running Count by 1½ to determine your Exact Count. That means a Running Count of +4 would convert to an Exact Count of +6 any time during the play of that second ¼ of the deck.

At the halfway point in the deck, with half the cards remaining to be dealt, the effect of each point of the Running Count is even greater. You now multiply by 2. Using a Running Count of +4 again, you would make the conversion by multiplying by 2 and you would have an Exact Count of +8.

Finally, when only the last ¼ of the deck remains to be dealt, you multiply by 4 to determine your Exact Count. In the same example, a Running Count of + 4 becomes an Exact Count of + 16.

Please note that you can calculate the Exact Count anytime you need it during play, but you *immediately return to the Running Count after your need for an Exact Count is over.* You use the Running Count to keep track of cards as the deck depletes, but you use the Exact Count only for certain key decisions.

Incidentally, there is nothing tricky about negative numbers when converting to the Exact Count: negative numbers in your Running Count convert easily.

For instance, a Running Count of − 4 becomes an Exact Count of − 8 at half the deck, and is therefore an even *smaller* number after the conversion. (There's a fuller explanation of how negative numbers work in chapter 3, table 8.) And, of course, 0 is always 0 no matter what you do to it.

Now that you know how to calculate the Exact Count, let's take a look at the enormous potential it gives your Expert System.

You learned in previous chapters how to beat single deck and double deck games against Las Vegas rules by using only the Running Count. Now, by learning how to convert that Running Count to an Exact Count you can vastly improve your play against those kinds of games with those kinds of rules. Even more important, by being able to figure the Exact Count, you can calculate your advantage so accurately you can go against single and double decks using almost any set of rules. And best of all, you will even be able to knock 'em dead playing against multiple decks, that innovation which was supposed to stop *all* counters! That's something you can't do with any degree of accuracy *without* employing the Exact Count.

So before we get into the stunning versatility of the Exact Count, let's take a look at how you convert the Running Count against multiple decks.

Multiple deck method

First, any time you are playing against more than one deck you mentally estimate the number of *single decks* remaining to be dealt. Then you *divide* your Running Count by the appropriate conversion figure to determine your advantage.

For instance, suppose you are playing against a four deck shoe. If the discard box contains one deck, then there are three decks remaining to be dealt. If there are two decks in the discard box, two remain to be dealt, etc. Now take a look at table 11 to find the right conversion figure.

TABLE 11

Converting Running Count to Exact Count with Multiple Decks

Number of Decks Remaining	Conversion Factor
6	Divide by 6
5	Divide by 5
4	Divide by 4
3	Divide by 3
2	Divide by 2
1	Divide by 1 (same as Running Count)

You can see, if you had a Running Count of +9 and there are three decks remaining to be dealt, you would divide by 3 to get an Exact Count of +3. Also, if you had a Running Count of −4 and there were two decks remaining, you would divide by 2 and have an Exact Count of −2.

The conversion figure of dividing by 2 against two decks remaining holds true whether you are playing against a four deck game with only two decks remaining, or simply starting out against a double deck game.

Now, when any number of multiple decks deplete to where only one deck remains, you use the single deck method of adjusting (multiply instead of divide).

At first all this sounds tough, but spend a few minutes and you'll see it's really pretty easy to remember (you memorize the table and

---

The Bad Old Days

Recently, Grinder told this story of playing in the old, unsophisticated days:

"In the early fifties I developed what I thought was a great system. It was a doozy, tougher than the devil to keep track of during play.

"First, I kept track of Aces by which notch in an ashtray I put my cigarette in. I counted fives by the angle of my foot on my chair rung. I kept track of the number of cards remaining, and the ratio of bigs to littles, by the way I arranged my chips. Meanwhile, my head was buzzing with strategies, indexes and ratios.

"During one play, a guy sat down and accidentally bumped my leg with his knee as he reached across and grabbed my ashtray. Pulling the ashtray back, he knocked over a stack of my chips. He apologized profusely.

"Unfortunately, my head was full as I was trying to keep track of everything, and I exploded.

'Boy, you're something,' I said. 'First you knock off my fives, then you grab my Aces and on top of that you bash down my ratio indicator . . . of all the. . . .

"About then I saw everyone thought I was crazy, so I cut it off. But you should have seen the looks!

"Those were tough days. Now the Expert Count does it all with one little set of numbers, the earning power is tripled, and the work involved is zilch.

"If I had known then what I know now, it wouldn't have taken me ten years to get my first million," he concluded ruefully.

---

don't take it into the casino). The key to the whole thing is simply: with any number of multiple decks, the number of decks remaining to be dealt from is the divisor, whether it's 2 decks, 4 decks, 8 decks, 80 decks, etc. Then, when the decks deplete to where only one remains, you use the single deck method and multiply.

So, with four decks remaining you divide your Running Count by 4 to get the Exact Count; with 3 decks remaining you divide by 3; with 2 remaining, divide by 2; with one deck remaining the Running Count and the Exact Count converge, or you multiply by 1; when ¾ of that deck is left, multiply by 1½; with half a deck multiply by 2; with ¼ left multiply by 4. Again, you estimate to the closest deck when whole decks remain, and to the nearest ¼ of a deck when only one deck remains.

As an example of how the Exact Count changes as various decks deplete, let's take a Running Count of +8 and follow it through all the conversions. If four decks remain, a Running Count of +8 converts to an Exact Count of +2 (8 divided by 4). If three decks remain, the Running Count converts to +3 (8 divided by 3, which would actually be +2⅔, but close enough). If two decks remain, the Exact Count becomes +4 (8 divided by 2).

Now on to the single deck method, or only one deck remaining. When one deck remains, the Exact Count is +8 (8 × 1). If ¾ of a single deck remains, the Running Count of +8 becomes an Exact Count of +12 (8 × 1½). If half of a single deck remains, the Exact Count is +16 (8 × 2). If ¼ of a single deck remains, the Exact Count is +32 (8 × 4).

And once again, you calculate the Exact Count anytime you need it, but immediately go back to the Running Count to keep track of cards.

Rule Variations and Betting Schedule

Now let's put the Exact Count to work to increase your playing punch. For openers, let's smash that bugaboo about only being able to play against certain kinds of rules and conditions. Here's the old one-two that'll do it:

1. Determine the house advantage, according to the rules it plays by.

2. Determine when your advantage overcomes the house advantage and increase your bet size at the point you have about a half a percent in your favor.

It's as easy as that. Here's how it looks in operation.

You remember that playing Basic Strategy against a single deck game with Las Vegas rules brought the house advantage down to .015 percent (a fifteen-thousandth of one percent) against you? Well, from that −.015 percent, add or subtract the Gain or Loss to Player figures from table 12 so you come up with an accurate disadvantage or advantage figure depending upon various house rules.

(The original rules were: You could double down on your first two cards, regardless of total; you could not double after splitting pairs; you could split any pair and re-split all pairs, except Aces; you could take Insurance; and the dealer had to hit 16 and stand on all 17's, including soft 17. These standard Las Vegas rules give the .015 percent against you.)

Here's most of the changes possible; simply total the gain or loss from the following chart:

TABLE 12

Approximate Effect on Player's Advantage
of Rule Variation for Basic Strategy

Rule Variation	Gain or Loss to Player (in percent)
Dealer draws to soft 17	−0.19
Four deck game	−0.50
Two deck game	−0.34
Six deck game	−0.60
Sixty deck game	−0.66
Doubling down forbidden on	
Hard 11	−0.89
Hard 10	−0.56
Hard 9	−0.14
Soft totals	−0.14
Permit doubling after pair splitting	+0.17
Permit doubling on three cards	+0.19
Permit doubling on any number of cards	+0.20
Further splitting of pairs	
All pairs except Aces	+0.02
All pairs including Aces	+0.05
Unlimited draw to split Aces	+0.14
Forbid splitting Aces	−0.16
Forbid splitting any pairs	−0.46
Surrender	+0.15
Two-to-one payoff on Blackjack	+2.33
No Blackjack bonus	−2.33

Credit

After you have established credit with a casino, you can then either cash checks at the cashier's cage to gamble with, or you can get chips at any table by asking a pit boss for them. He will give you the chips, check with the cage to see that you haven't exceeded your limit, and have you sign what amounts to a check for the amount you receive . . . not necessarily in that order.

If you should win, you are usually expected to pick up your markers before you leave the table. If you should lose, the markers are debited to your account in the cage.

If you plan on playing at the "high roller" level, you will probably want to establish credit in one or more casinos.

To get familiar with the operation, let's take as an example a very unfavorable set of rules you might find in the Reno area (if you looked hard enough) and do the figuring. We'll treat the rule variations of table 12 as being added or subtracted from zero, as the −0.015 percent against you using standard Las Vegas rules is simply not significant enough to warrant carrying that figure and dealing with it three places beyond the decimal point.

Rule Variation Example, #1

Rule	Gain or Loss to Player
Two deck game	−0.34 percent
Dealer draws to soft 17	−0.19
Doubling down forbidden on:	
Hard 9	−0.14
Soft totals	−0.14
	Total −0.81

Now that you know what the house advantage is, you only need to figure the point you overcome it with your Exact Count. Here's the info to enable you to do it.

TABLE 13

Player's Approximate Advantage for
Various Exact Counts

Exact Count	Player's Approximate Advantage (in percent)
8	4.0
7	3.5
6	3.0
5	2.5
4	2.0
3	1.5
2	1.0
1	.5
0	0
−1	−.5
−2	−1.0
−3	−1.5
−4	−2.0
−5	−2.5
−6	−3.0
−7	−3.5
−8	−4.0

You can see that for each plus point of the Exact Count, your advantage increases by one half of a percent (0.5%). So, at +6 you have gained about three percent. Or at +8, you've gained about four percent. Conversely, at −8, you have about four percent against you.

You'll notice the table only shows the advantage or disadvantage of Exact Counts from +8 to −8, a sufficient range to get the idea. You'll be happy to know, though, that as the Exact Count goes higher your advantage continues to increase and may approach 100 percent. But as the Exact Count becomes more negative, your disadvantage, or the House's advantage—does not exceed approximately five percent.

Back to rule variation example #1. We figured you had −.81 percent against you with those rules; at what point do you overcome that? Table 13, the chart which shows your increase in advantage for various Exact Counts, tells you that at an Exact Count of +2 you have gained a full percent (1.0%), and that is enough to overcome −.81%. However, since −.81% subtracted from 1.0% only equals .19% (about a twentieth of one percent), that is not really sufficiently great enough an advantage to capitalize upon. Our general rule is to try and get about a full half a percent (.5%) in your favor before increasing bet size.

But at an Exact Count of +3, you've gained a full half a percent plus, and that's a nice safe place to start increasing your bet size (+3 equals a gain of 1.5%; −.81% from that and you get .69%).

Apology time

Up to this chapter in the book, we suggested you bet with your Running Count at +2 when playing Basic Strategy against single decks using Las Vegas and Reno-Lake Tahoe rules, and against double decks using Las Vegas rules only.

We did that to get you out playing—and winning—early, without going into a lot of detail. But now that you *have* the details, you can see that betting with the Running Count doesn't always maximize your win potential.

For instance, against a single deck using Las Vegas rules, your disadvantage is only −0.015 percent. Therefore, at an Exact Count of +1 your increase in advantage (table 13) of .5 percent gives you almost a half a percent in your favor (.5% −.015% =.485%). That's close enough to a half a percent advantage, so with those rules you can start increasing your bets at an Exact Count of +1. In other words, you can bet *two* chips at +1, three chips at +2, and your suggested maximum bet of four chips at +3.

Another apology

On the other hand, figure the odds on the double deck game

using only Las Vegas rules. Here your Rule Variation chart (table 12) tells you the only increase in disadvantage over a Vegas single deck game is −.34%, due to the use of two decks.

We suggested you bet two units at a Running Count of +2 against this game. Since that translates to an Exact Count of +1 at the beginning of two-deck play (table 11), you have only gained .5 percent which, when you subtract the above −.34 percent, gives you a sparse .16 percent in your favor. You won't get hurt with that, but it's better to have *at least* a quarter percent in your favor before betting (to reduce fluctuation) or, better yet, a full half a percent.

So, to be safer, when playing against double decks, Las Vegas rules, don't jump from a one unit to a two unit bet until you have an Exact Count of +2 (Running Count of +4—table 11). That way, you have better than a full half a percent in your favor (an Exact Count of +2 gives you a gain of 1 percent. Double deck game, Las Vegas rules, gives the player a disadvantage of −.34 percent. Take −.34 percent from 1 percent and you have a .66 percent advantage).

No apology here

Though you overbet your advantage a little with double decks, and underbet it a little with single decks, Las Vegas rules, in the case of single decks with Reno-Lake Tahoe rules you were right on the money. Here are the rules: Doubling forbidden on hard 9 (−.14 percent); doubling forbidden on soft totals (−.14 percent).

Since the Exact Count and the Running Count are the same for the first quarter of a single deck (table 10), this one is very easy to figure. With a count of +1, you have gained .5 percent, but when you subtract −.28 percent for Reno rules you only end up with .22 percent in your favor. You would like at least a quarter of a percent, and better yet, a full half a percent. By waiting until +2 before betting two units, you've achieved better than half a percent in your favor.

When worst comes to worst

I mentioned earlier that Vegas, frightened by Thorp, changed the rules for a few weeks back in 1964. By doing this, they drove

---

Meet the Dealer

Most books would have you believe that dealers are a beady-eyed bunch who are anxious to win (if not cheat) against every player (and especially counters) who comes in. I'd like you to meet a few of the dealers on my shift, tonight. Come on in and take a look around.

There's Paul. He's frowning and he's mad. I corrected him twice so far tonight, once for overpaying a customer, once for underpaying. He got drunk after his shift yesterday and didn't quite get enough sleep before coming in. He's going to be surly the whole shift because he figures I'm on his back.

Over there is Delores. She has a bad corn on her right foot and is wearing uncomfortably high heels for a date after shift tonight. She will dance all night and come in tomorrow with even sorer feet.

Back there stands Jack. He's a toke hustler. Tucks the card under the customer's double-down money and says, "Good luck on that, sir." If the customer wins and doesn't tip, the next time a big bet goes out he pauses and cocks his head and frowns. He lets you know in a jillion tiny ways he's in on your action when you're winning. When you're losing, he deals faster so maybe you get gone and a big tipper will sit down.

Now take Charlie over there. Been in the business 20 years, can deal competently in his sleep, and I think he does. Never

(Continued)

---

away regular customers, but didn't stop our Dynamic Duo. Here's the rule changes, and how Grinder and Hungry overcame them: doubling forbidden on all totals except 11; no splitting Aces.

It doesn't *sound* like much, but you can see from table 12 that these changes give the house about a full one percent advantage. You can also see from table 13, that all Grinder and Hungry had to do was wait until their Exact Count was +3 (overcoming the house advantage of 1 percent and capturing a half a percent for themselves) before increasing their bets.

At that point, it was business as usual. The only difference was that they now waited until +3 to bet two units.

Meet the Dealer (Cont.)

changes expression, win, lose, toke or stiff. However, his voice rises slightly in tone and volume when he thanks someone for a tip.

To my left is Chitty Chatty Bang Bang. She's doing her best to be unapproachable and uncommunicative with everyone at her table. She lost her last three jobs for striking up conversations with male customers, dating them and. . . . Well, that's how she got her nickname. She doesn't want to make the same mistake here.

Down the end is Marcus the Mad Adder. Whenever he hits his own hand three times he pays the whole table, no matter what his own total is. He simply cannot, or will not, add up hands logically. The big boss hired him and I have to watch his table very closely. He always looks like he's concentrating very hard, to throw me off.

I singled out just these six to make a point. Everyone of them would look formidable to a new counter. They all look like they are serious and right on top of everything. They all have odd moments when they frown or look contemplative or suddenly change the pace of their game or do something out of synch.

Not one of them could tell a card counter from a lunch counter.

They are people standing on their feet doing a job for pay which is basically assembly-line work. Most people they deal to treat them as if they're a beady-eyed bunch who are anxious to win against everyone who comes in.

Let the games begin

You can now win against just about any Blackjack game anywhere. Simply calculate the house odds against you (table 12), then determine at what plus count your Exact Count overcomes those odds (table 13). You must use the *Exact Count* (tables 10 and 11) to do this. Then start increasing your bets when you have at least a quarter percent, and preferably a half a percent, in your favor.

After that, the best way to establish your Ideal Bet Size (the amount you would *like* to bet, in proportion to your advantage) is to add one more unit for each plus point of the Exact Count.

If for instance, you are playing against a certain Puerto Rican casino where you don't increase your bet to two units until +4, you would then: bet three units at +5, and four units at +6, etc. That is, if it would look natural to do so.

When best comes to best

Naturally, all these details are useful to help you play no matter how tough casinos attempt to make the game. But take another look at table 12 and add up all the possible advantages you can acquire as a result of liberal rules.

Fantastic!

You can see you actually have a nice advantage which might start at 0, or even minus counts. With that kind of game, you can win with Basic Strategy alone, and without increasing the size of your bets at all! How sweet can it be?

Impossible? No, definitely not. At the time of this writing, there are three casinos in Nevada alone which have such liberal rules (to attract players) that Basic Strategy—without even keeping track of cards—will make you a winner.

Still, *I'd* feel obligated to keep track and move my money up a little on the plus side just to cut down my playing time—I could use that time to improve my golf stroke.

Tiny review

Learn how to figure the Exact Count for added power against any game you wish to play (tables 10 and 11).

With the Exact Count you can then figure at what point your increase in advantage (table 13) overcomes the house advantage (table 12).

Then you use your Exact Count to begin increasing bets at the point your advantage overcomes the house advantage (that is, when you have a quarter to a half a percent in your favor).

Though you are now using the Exact Count for betting, you always maintain a Running Count to keep track of cards as they are dealt.

More simply, you always keep a Running Count, but now you will convert it to an Exact Count in the lull between hands to figure very accurately what the Ideal size of your next bet should be.

You will still modify your Ideal Bet Size according to SPY, Sly

---

Accuracy?

Some Blackjack writers have contributed greatly to the general confusion concerning strategies by claiming their systems are extremely "accurate." While "accuracy" in any endeavor sounds like a desirable and all-encompassing term, when describing a count strategy it really applies in three distinctly separate and major areas:

1) Efficiency in determining favorability, or bet size.
2) Efficiency in determining playing strategy.
3) Efficiency in actual use–in other words, practicality.

These three factors taken together, determine the total efficiency of a system.

If you'd like to end all of the arguments once and for all, and see how all of the popular systems on the market today compare, see our offer of the Special Report on Blackjack Systems *in chapter 7.*

Proportional Yields, as described in chapter 4. However, as you review that material, remember that two significant things have changed:

1. You are now betting your money according to the Exact Count and *not* the Running Count.

2. You now know how to increase your bets against any kind of game, not just single and double deck games as described earlier. Therefore, you can start moving your money any time the Exact Count calls for it and it looks right.

Suggested betting limits

Since you are now betting with the Exact Count, your playing power has increased enormously and it's time to refine your betting spread a bit. For one thing, you will henceforth be pushing out a lot more money more quickly on which you have the advantage. A major caution, therefore, is to make sure it's not obvious you are *only* making larger bets when you have the edge.

For single deck games, we still suggest a maximum betting spread of from 1 to 4 units, even using the Exact Count. You can jump to a bigger spread of from 1 to 5 or more if you wish. However, dealers tend to shuffle-up more frequently or assume you are counting if your betting spread becomes too great. Until you have experience, stick with 1 to 4 units against single decks.

When you play against four deck shoes using Las Vegas rules, you have an approximate disadvantage of ½ of one percent at the start of the shoe. (This is due in part to the fact that you get fewer Naturals with four decks than with one deck.) So don't increase your bets until you have an Exact Count of +2.

Also, since casinos are less concerned about counters beating the shoe, you can spread your bets from 1 to 6 units or more, depending upon how observant casino personnel are. If you wish to bet 8, 10 or more units in favorable situations, you can always spread out to two hands, placing half your total bet on each hand.

For example, say you're going to bet 8 units. You may then bet two hands of four units each. However, remember you must have an Exact Count of +8 in order to justify the 8 unit bet.

As a general rule, use a betting spread of from 1 to 6 units when playing against a four-deck shoe. After you have gained enough experience to judge how far you can spread without alerting casino personnel, increase your betting spread to whatever the traffic will bear, just as you would with any game—if your bankroll justifies it (chapter 4).

Two deck games are now on the increase in Las Vegas, and many other places where only single decks were dealt before. The betting schedule for these games is essentially the same as for single decks, the exception being that you can generally increase your top bet without suspicion to five units instead of four, using the Exact Count.

Since there are some inherent disadvantages in playing against multiple decks (as opposed to single decks), you will generally have to maintain a larger betting spread in order to enjoy the same return.

Modifying Basic—The Numbers Game

The Basic Strategy presented in chapter 2 is the correct way to play your hand without counting. Basic takes into consideration a player's initial two cards and the dealer's upcard. However, as the

---

Clocking Your Play

You can find a game any time of the day or night in almost any Nevada casino. With three shifts too choose from, it's not difficult to find a spot at your convenience.

But in most foreign casinos you have to do a little scheduling. The majority of them post hours for play, often six or twelve hours a day, which ends usually between two and four in the morning. Some will stay open as long as the action warrants it, but one or two players are frequently not considered enough action.

Check on local conditions and allow yourself adequate time to get the job done. It's not fun to get caught with your big bet out just when they turn out the lights.

---

deck depletes, composition of the remaining cards continually changes. Since the Expert Count measures these changes to an amazingly accurate degree, you can often improve upon Basic Strategy to increase your overall gain by appropriately using the deck composition information the Expert Count gives you.

An excess of high cards remaining (or a shortage of low cards) makes itself known by a plus, or positive, count. Conversely, an excess of low cards remaining (or a shortage of high cards) makes itself known by a minus, or negative, count.

Thus when your Exact Count is positive (+), you should generally stand a little more often (and let the dealer break); and you should double down and split more often (you make more hands *and* the dealer tends to break more).

When your Exact Count is negative (−), you should generally draw more frequently (to make a hand, since the dealer will also have more successful draws with more little cards in the deck); and double down and split less often (you are less likely to make a good hand *and* the dealer will make more hands).

Of course you'll still be using Basic most of the time (about 80 percent). But as the deck depletes, you'll find numerous situations which will work greatly to your advantage by altering Basic. This is another place the Exact Count really shines, for it provides utmost accuracy for making those decision changes.

So you'll get the most advantage—and money—for the energy you expend adding on these techniques, we'll take a look at the hit-stand, doubling and pair splitting strategies in just that order—their order of percentage increase to you.

Tables 14 and 15 show the hit-stand decisions, the most important aspect of modifying Basic.

TABLE 14

Modifying Basic Strategy:
Expert Hard Hit–Stand Decisions

Your Hard Total	Dealer's Up Card									
	2	**3**	**4**	**5**	**6**	**7**	**8**	**9**	**10**	**A**
12	2	1	0	−2	−1	H	H	H	H	H
13	−1	−2	−3	−5	−5	H	H	H	H	H
14	−4	−5	−6	S	S	H	H	H	H	H
15	−6	S	S	S	S	H	H	H	4	H
16	S	S	S	S	S	H	H	5	0	H
17–21	S	S	S	S	S	S	S	S	S	S

S = *Always Stand*
H = *Always Hit (draw to hand)*

All other decisions are determined by the Exact Count. Stand if the Exact Count is equal to or larger than the number in the square. Hit if the Exact Count is less than the number in the square.

To figure the decisions, look in the square which is intersected by going across the column from your hard total and down from the dealer's upcard. If the square has an "S" or an "H", you simply stand or hit; there is no change from Basic. But if the square contains a number, you stand only if the Exact Count (*not* the Running Count) is equal to or greater than that number.

For example, if you have a hard 12 and the dealer has a 2 for an upcard, you stand if your Exact Count is +2 or more, otherwise you hit. Previously, you always hit with Basic against this hand.

But now that you know how to figure the Exact Count, and therefore know true deck composition, you can gain a little extra edge by not hitting at +2 or higher (with a higher proportion of high cards in the deck, you are in effect saving those cards for the dealer to break with).

TABLE 15

Modifying Basic Strategy: Expert Soft Hit–Stand Decisions

Your Soft Total	Dealer's Up Card									
	2	3	4	5	6	7	8	9	10	A
18	S	S	S	S	S	S	S	H	H	0
19 or Higher	S	S	S	S	S	S	S	S	S	S

S = *Always Stand*
H = *Always Hit*

The only change from Basic is soft 18 vs. a dealer upcard of Ace. Stand if the Exact Count is zero or higher; hit if Exact Count is minus one or lower.

Another example; note that you stand with 13 against a 4 at −3 or higher. That means you would hit at −4 or lower (−5, −6, −7, −8, etc.). Here your Exact Count has told you it is more to your advantage to hit and make a hand (which is what the dealer is likely to do with an excess of low cards in the deck), rather than stand.

When using the negative number decisions, remember that a decision which calls for standing at −2 or *higher* means you would stand at −2, −1, 0, +1, +2, +3, +4, etc. Conversely, you would then be hitting at numbers *lower* than −2, which are: −3, −4, −5, −6, −7, −8, etc.

Negative numbers tend to confuse some people, but just remember that minus numbers grow *smaller* as they seem to get larger. Thus, −10 is a lower number than −9; and −6 is a higher number than -7. If this is confusing, it might help to review table 8 in chapter 3 which graphically shows you how you get farther from plus numbers the more you move into minus numbers.

TABLE 16
Modifying Basic Strategy: Expert Hard Doubling

Your Hard Total	Dealer's Up Card									
	2	3	4	5	6	7	8	9	10	A
8	H	H	6	4	3	H	H	H	H	H
9	1	0	-2	-5	-5	4	H	H	H	H
10	D	D	D	D	D	D	-5	-2	6	5
11	D	D	D	D	D	D	-6	-5	-3	1

H = Always Hit
D = Always Double

Double down if the Exact Count is equal to or greater than the number in the square, otherwise do not double.

The Exact Count in action

Now that you have the decisions, lets take a look at the Exact Count in action for both betting and modifying Basic Strategy.

When using the card count information to vary your strategy for playing hands, count each card as it is exposed, using the Running Count. Soon as you see your first two cards and the dealer's upcard, count them. As each player draws cards, keep an up-to-the-second Running Count total. If you must draw to your hand, include the cards drawn in your Running Count total. If the hit-stand decisions requires you to convert to an Exact Count, do so at your turn of play.

Now we'll put it all together. Suppose you are playing against a four deck shoe, Las Vegas rules, and you are down to the last deck. The last round has just been completed and the dealer is ready to deal a new round. Approximately 26 cards remain (½ deck) to be dealt and your Running Count is +3.

TABLE 17

Modifying Basic Strategy:
Expert Soft Doubling

Your Soft Hand	Dealer's Up Card				
	2	3	4	5	6
A, 2	H	H	3	−1	−2
A, 3	H	6	2	−2	−5
A, 4	H	5	−1	−5	D
A, 5	H	4	−1	−6	D
A, 6	1	−2	−6	D	D
A, 7	2	−1	−6	D	D
A, 8	S	5	4	2	2
A, 9	S	S	S	S	S

H = Always Hit
D = Always Double
S = Always Stand

Double down if the Exact Count is equal to or greater than the number in the square; otherwise do not double.

The first thing you do is establish your bet size. To do this, you must compute the Exact Count. Since your Running Count is +3 and ½ a deck remains, your Exact Count is +6 (2 × 3). You may bet 6 units on the next hand (our suggested maximum against a shoe). Now that you've used the Exact Count where it was needed, drop back to the Running Count of +3 and keep the Running Count in your head to keep track of cards.

Say the dealer now receives a 9 for an upcard. Your Running Count goes to +2. You look at your initial two cards and see a 3 and a 4. Your Running Count becomes +4. The player to your right draws a 10. Your Running Count goes to +3. He draws again and receives a 9. Your Running Count becomes +2. He broke and turns over his two cards, both dueces. These are zero-value cards so your Running Count stays +2. It is now your turn to draw.

TABLE 18

Modifying Basic Strategy: Expert Pair Splitting
(Doubling after Splits Not Permitted)

Your Pair	Dealer's Up Card									
	2	3	4	5	6	7	8	9	10	A
2, 2	H	2	−4	Sp	Sp	Sp	H	H	H	H
3, 3	H	5	0	−2	Sp	Sp	H	H	H	H
4, 4										
5, 5										
6, 6	3	0	−1	−5	−6	H	H	H	H	H
7, 7	Sp	Sp	Sp	Sp	Sp	Sp	H	H	H	H
8, 8	Sp	Sp	Sp	Sp	Sp	Sp	Sp	Sp	Sp	Sp
9, 9	−1	−2	−3	−5	−3	S	Sp	Sp	S	S
10, 10	S	S	S	5	5	S	S	S	S	S
A, A	Sp	Sp	Sp	Sp	Sp	Sp	Sp	Sp	Sp	−5

Sp = *Always Split*
S = *Always Stand*
H = *Always Hit*

Split if the Exact Count is equal to or greater than the number in the square, otherwise do not split.
Do not split 4, 4 or 5, 5.

Since your hand totals hard 7 (a 3 and a 4), you do not have to convert your Running Count of +2 to the Exact Count as you always draw to hard 7. Suppose you draw a 5 spot. Your hand totals 12 and your Running Count becomes +3. Since you always draw to hard 12 versus a dealer's upcard of 9, you motion for another card without having to compute an Exact Count. You draw a 4 spot. Your hand now totals hard 16 and your Running Count becomes +4.

At this point you must convert your Running Count to an Exact Count to determine whether or not to draw to hard 16 versus the dealer's upcard 9. You find your Exact Count is +8 (Running

TABLE 19

*Modifying Basic Strategy: Expert Pair Splitting
(Doubling after Splits Permitted)*

Your Pair	Dealer's Up Card									
	2	**3**	**4**	**5**	**6**	**7**	**8**	**9**	**10**	**A**
2, 2	−5	−6	Sp	Sp	Sp	Sp	H	H	H	H
3, 3	−2	Sp	Sp	Sp	Sp	Sp	H	H	H	H
4, 4	H	H	4	2	0	H	H	H	H	H
5, 5										
6, 6	−1	−3	−5	Sp	Sp	H	H	H	H	H
7, 7	Sp	Sp	Sp	Sp	Sp	Sp	−1	H	H	H
8, 8	Sp	Sp	Sp	Sp	Sp	Sp	Sp	Sp	Sp	Sp
9, 9	−3	−4	−6	Sp	−6	4	Sp	Sp	S	5
10, 10	S	S	S	5	5	S	S	S	S	S
A, A	Sp	Sp	Sp	Sp	Sp	Sp	Sp	Sp	Sp	−5

Sp = Always Split
S = Always Stand
H = Always Hit

*Split if the Exact Count is equal to or greater
than the number in the square, otherwise do
not split.*

Do not split 5, 5.

Count of +4 × 2, at half a deck), and you stand according to table 14. This chart shows that you stand with hard 16 against a 9 at +5 or more.

Note you do not use the Running Count to make strategy decisions; you are using the Exact Count. Then, after you convert to an Exact Count for specific betting or strategy decisions, drop immediately back to your Running Count and continue to maintain it.

Finally, when the dealer re-shuffles the deck, kill the Running Count and start the new deck with a count of zero.

Review on learning to modify basic

Mastering the hit-stand and hard doubling-down decisions will account for most of the gain you can derive from modifying Basic Strategy. Learn those first, and while learning, use Basic for any playing decisions you are not absolutely certain of. When you are intimate friends with hit-stand and hard doubling, start adding the soft-doubling and pair-splitting strategies to your bag of tricks— also in that order.

We have not given all possible changes to the Basic Strategy that a card counter can employ, but these are the most important. The average player learning how to count would be overwhelmed by more material than we have presented in these charts. Our primary purpose is to make you a winning player, not turn you into a walking memory bank.

Concentrate on mastering the charts and material presented in this book. The inherent patterns in the charts should help make memorizing easier. When you have accomplished that, and should you wish to go even further, chapter 7 will show you how.

Insurance

Taking Insurance provides one of the easiest jumps in playing power when using the Exact Count. When the Exact Count is +2 or more, you definitely take Insurance. If the Exact Count is less than +2, you should not take it. The reason is simple and mathematically bulletproof—the higher the plus count, the greater the amount of tens remaining (on average) in the undealt portion, and the higher the dealer's probability of having a Blackjack.

It works like this. A full deck of 52 cards consists of 36 non-tens and 16 tens. Assuming the dealer has an Ace up (and temporarily ignoring the player's initial two cards) the odds are 35 to 16, or 2.19 to 1, that he does not have a ten count card in the hole. Since the house offers 2 to 1 odds on Insurance, the player who takes Insurance in this instance has a disadvantage of 5.9 percent.

As the deck depletes, the ratio of tens to non-tens continuously changes. If the ratio of non-tens to tens is exactly 2 to 1, neither player nor house has an advantage on the Insurance bet. When the ratio is greater than 2 to 1, the house has the advantage. Any time the ratio of non-tens to tens is less than 2 to 1, you have a favorable bet.

Most players and casino personnel share the common mis-conception that you should always insure a Blackjack. Their rea-soning is that if you insure the Blackjack, you win the amount of your original bet (with no bonus) whether the dealer has a Natural or not, and are thus a "sure" winner. Remember, though, you forfeit the extra bonus Blackjack pays when you insure, since the dealer takes your Insurance bet (half your original bet) when he doesn't have a Natural.

A variation of this misconception assumes you should insure a "good" hand and not insure a "bad" hand against an Ace. Like most fallacies surrounding Insurance, you can shoot that one down easily, too.

Suppose you are counting down the deck and realize no ten count cards remain. If the dealer has an Ace up you probably wouldn't take Insurance unless someone had a gun to your head: the dealer couldn't possibly have a Blackjack. On the other hand, if all remaining cards were ten count cards, you have that rarity of all bets, a 100% cinch—the dealer must have a Blackjack.

So in the first example you couldn't possibly win the Insurance bet; in the second you couldn't lose. It had nothing to do with your own "good" or "bad" hand, but was strictly a result of whether the deck held all tens or no tens.

Now, somewhere between no tens remaining and a deck con-sisting of all tens, there is a point where the odds begin to tip in your favor. That is at an Exact Count of +2 or higher, and that is where you take Insurance. And since you are using the Exact Count, the same rule of +2 applies to single decks, double decks, or any other multiple deck combination.

Adjusting for Aces

You can squeeze in even more accuracy when determining your correct, or Ideal, bet size by adjusting the Exact Count to compen-sate for an excess or shortage of Aces. Do this by keeping a separate side count of Aces as they are played from the deck. But caution: while adjusting for Aces gives a little extra edge, tackle this refinement last; it tends to be difficult. The details will still be here later when you are ready for them.

Since you value the Ace as a neutral card in the Expert System,

---

The Old Counting Wheeze

Most Blackjack counters are an amusing lot. They spend a lot of time worrying about being caught, but for no reason. See, most of them can't beat the game! They are living in the past with old-time systems, old-time betting strategies and old-time rules.

The average counter expects to bet one unit through all the situations where he has no advantage, then jump his bet as high as he can when the cards turn and he has the advantage. Let me tell you what happens when someone plays like that.

Nothing!

Of course the dealer may shuffle by reflex, to show the bosses he is on his toes, but often he will not–unless he is at the point he would normally shuffle anyway. By shuffling, the dealer knows the odds on the next hand go to about even and neither house nor player has an advantage with Basic Strategy.

What has really happened is that the "counter" has shown the dealer that he is subject to make a big bet when a lot of little cards come out.

Now, if he continues to jump his bet up drastically every time little cards come out, and only when little cards come out, he's advertising that he has read some old-timer's book and is trying to be a counter. He is also making problems for everyone.

For instance, the dealer usually doesn't care who does what to whom . . . as long as he doesn't get caught in the middle. He can't afford to have his bosses think he's so stupid he can't shuffle the cards when someone makes a monster bet following a string of minimum bets.

So the dealer begins shuffling everytime the "counter" puts a big bet out. If the dealer is a red-hot, and wants to move up to

(Continued)

---

the Exact Count automatically determines the correct modifications to your strategy for the play of any hand (hit-stand, double down, split). Exceptions are rare and insignificant in overall play return. However, the betting strategy (as determined by the Exact Count) assumes a normal amount of Aces remain in undealt cards. (A normal amount of Aces is defined as one Ace remaining for every thirteen cards left to be dealt.) Inasmuch as the number of Aces remaining sometimes deviates from normal, if you

---

The Old Counting Wheeze (Cont.)

floorman or pit boss, he will tell someone over him how smart he is and that he has "caught" a counter in action.

The alleged counter has now lobbed a boulder in the pond and the ripples spread out to rock everybody's boat. The dealer feels he has to be on his toes because the guy is obvious and has probably already caught the attention of the bosses.

The bosses see the dealer is alerted and cannot afford to look any less sharp than the hired hands.

The counter sees everyone is stirred up and is now playing under the pressure of a lot of people scrutinizing him and his play.

Incredible!

This alleged "counter" has shown he can't even beat the game, for the first requisite to winning at Blackjack is getting the cards dealt to you when you have an advantage. Yet, even though he can't beat the game, he has managed to put a lot of pressure on everyone.

The problem is that most would-be counters play so badly and obviously that they tip off their play.

The solution is to play a strong system well enough to look like an average player.

It's a question of goals. If you want to make money playing the game, do it our way. If you want recognition as being as "super-smart" as the average system seller, play like they do and you will get the notoriety they strive so hard for. If you want to make money outside the casinos, join the legion of losers who are suing for not being allowed to play (a lot of indignant system sellers in this group, too).

It's a question of goals.

---

compensate for the excess or shortage you can determine the degree of favorability more precisely for any Exact Count. And that means you can get even more accurate with your betting.

In general, if there is a shortage of Aces remaining in the undealt cards, the deck is less favorable than the Exact Count correlation on the table titled, "Player's Approximate Advantage for Various Exact Counts" (table 13).

Conversely, if the deck contains a surplus of Aces, the deck is more favorable than the Exact Count correlation suggests. One reason is that the chance of getting a Natural (with that bonus payoff!) is increased.

You can compensate for the effect of an excess or shortage of Aces quite accurately. Table 20 shows the effect on the Exact Count of each Ace deviating from normal for various amounts of cards remaining.

TABLE 20
Effect of Aces

Number of Decks Remaining	Value of Each Ace Deviating from Normal
6	$^1/_6$
5	$^1/_5$
4	$^1/_4$
3	$^1/_3$
2	$^1/_2$
1	1
$^1/_2$	2
$^1/_4$	4

To restate the above chart, if ½ deck remains to be dealt, each Ace in excess of normal increases the Exact Count by 2 points *for betting*.

If one deck remains, each Ace above or below normal increases or decreases the Exact Count by one point. If three decks remain to be dealt, each Ace above or below normal increases or decreases the Exact Count by ⅓ point (it takes an excess or shortage of three Aces to change the Exact Count by one point when three decks remain). Note we are talking about the Exact Count, not the Running Count.

As an example to help clarify the difference, let's assume 26 cards remain to be dealt (or ½ deck remaining) and your Running

Count is +1. What is the correct Exact Count for betting purposes? Here's a rundown.

If a normal amount of Aces remain (two Aces), your Exact Count for betting purposes is +2 (you multiply your Running Count of +1 by the factor of 2 to get the Exact Count at ½ deck).

Suppose however, the deck contained one extra Ace (a total of three Aces remaining, instead of the expected two). The Exact Count for betting would be +4. You arrive at this adjusted Exact Count by taking the original Exact Count of +2 and adding to it 2 points for the extra Ace at the 26 card level, since the deck is more favorable due to an excess Ace.

Then again, suppose the deck contained no Aces (two Aces short at the 26 card level), and the Running Count was +1; our adjusted Exact Count would be −2 for betting purposes. You arrive at this figure by multiplying the Running Count (+1) by the Exact Count factor (2) to get an Exact Count of +2. But since you are short two Aces, you now subtract 4 (2 points for each Ace short) from the Exact Count to arrive at an adjusted Exact Count of −2 (2 −4= −2). In this instance, the shortage of Aces nullified your advantage and made the deck unfavorable for betting.

As you can see from the above examples, the deviation of Aces from normal can have a pronounced effect on the degree of favorability for betting purposes. *However, please keep in mind that you do not adjust your Exact Count to reflect an excess or shortage of Aces when you make hit-stand, doubling and pair splitting decisions.* You only adjust the Exact Count for Aces to gain greater accuracy in determining Ideal Bet Size.

Once you have made your Exact Count adjustment to reflect an excess or shortage of Aces for betting, revert to the original Running Count and continue with play.

Practically speaking, adjusting for Aces is more important in single deck play than in multiple deck games. The effect of Ace deviation when playing against a four deck shoe is usually negligible when 3 or 4 decks remain to be played. However, it can become important when the shoe has depleted to 1½ decks or less.

As an example, with four decks remaining, it requires an excess or shortage of four Aces to change the Exact Count by one point (each Ace counts ¼ point at the 4 deck level); with three decks remaining, it requires an excess or shortage of three Aces to change the Exact Count by one point (each Ace counts ⅓ point at the three deck level). Therefore, unless the number of Aces swings greatly out of line, the effect of a deviation at the three and four deck level is usually insignificant.

However, when the multiple deck comes down to about the one deck level, an excess or shortage of Aces can be more significant, although often this deviation will not affect your betting.

For example, suppose one deck remains to be played and eight Aces remain in the undealt cards (four extra Aces). If the Running Count was +2, the four extra Aces would enable you to make a much larger bet. Your adjusted Exact Count would be +6 (2 × 1 + 4). However, if the Running Count was +8 instead of +2, the fact that the extra Aces remained would not enable you to increase your bet, since you would be making your maximum bet anyway.

Of course, if the deck were negative, a *shortage* of Aces would not change your bet, since you would be making your minimum bet anyway.

Again, only after you have played the Expert System for some time and can easily and accurately keep a Running Count, convert to an Exact Count, bet your money properly, and make correct playing decisions by modifying Basic Strategy, should you attempt to keep a separate count of Aces.

At that point, make it easy on yourself and work gradually into keeping track of Aces. When the deck has an excess of Aces, bet a little more in favorable situations, as you know the deck is slightly more favorable than the Exact Count suggests. If there's a shortage of Aces, decrease bets a bit to compensate. Keep in mind that the Aces affect favorability more as you get closer to the bottom of the deck, and that *estimating* the effect of Aces is almost as good as making a precise calculation.

After you have sufficient experience compensating generally, you may then wish to attempt to very accurately adjust for Aces by using the precise figures in table 20. Correctly compensating for Aces increases your betting efficiency to the optimum practical level.

Incidentally, this technique of adjusting for cards which are not included in your Running Count is known in math circles as a "multi-parameter" approach. Your Expert system lends itself more readily to this technique than any other system.

If card counting is easy for you, do keep a side count of Aces and adjust your betting accordingly. Every little bit helps. But if playing the count requires a great deal of effort, don't attempt a side count of Aces until you are doing everything else easily. The additional effort can cause you to make errors in play which may more than cancel out the slight gain that compensating for Aces gives you.

When Do You Surrender?

I know that last bit was a mind-bender, but I'm not suggesting you give up. "Surrender" is a critter offered in some casinos; and when you know how to use it you can get another chunk of gain fairly easily.

These casinos allow you to toss in, or Surrender, your initial two-card starting hand by paying half of your original bet to the dealer (you take the other half back). You must Surrender your hand prior to drawing any additional cards, and you cannot Surrender if the dealer has a Blackjack. Here's the strategy:

TABLE 21

Expert Surrender
Strategy

Your Hard Total	Dealer's Up Card		
	9	10	A
14		4	
15	3	−1	1
16	2	−2	0
8, 8		3	

Surrender if the Exact Count is equal to or greater than the number in the square, otherwise do not Surrender.

Do not Surrender if square is blank.

Junkets

This is the very best way to cut the nut (slash expenses). Many major hotel-casinos regularly fly in planeloads of their best gambling customers gratis, and likewise pick up the tab for RFB (room, food, and beverages). This service can be found in almost any major city in the country.

The only conditions are that the customer have good credit, will gamble at a reasonably high rate and for a reasonably long period of time. He doesn't have to lose, he only has to be an active gambler.

Most of the time the customer is expected to put up front money, either a cash deposit or a letter of credit to show his checks will be good.

Rule of thumb: If you put up $5,000, you can expect a free round-trip jet from the East and RFB for about four days.

It's not too tough to get on a junket, but it is tough to do it the right way. All of the Vegas hotels have been ripped off repeatedly by people who fly in and stay for free and never gamble.

The marginal ways to get on a junket include: writing the major

(Continued)

While it might sound strange to give up half your bet without playing your hand, the logic is faultless: if you have a *greater* than 50 percent chance of losing your bet, you are better off giving up 50 percent.

WHAT COMES NEXT

There's nothing heavy left!

If you haven't already read the next chapter, "The Expert's Guide to Keeping Your Name on the Welcome Mat," you have some valuable—and non-technical—material to look forward to. Then, in the last chapter, find details on the Master System, if you're curious, and a few other tid-bits you might be interested in.

So do push on to the lighter stuff; and don't get carried away with trying to master this whole Advanced chapter in one sitting— you're supposed to be taking it bit by bit as you feel up to it. After

---

Junkets (Cont.)

casinos directly and inquiring; taking a list of junketeers and contacting them; going through the phone book or newspapers.

These are all marginal because you're going in "cold." They don't know you and they are worried you might not be a big enough gambler to warrant getting big comps.

The best way, and the toughest, is to know someone. Usually a junketmaster (the guy who finds customers and fills planes for the casinos) is either a bookie or in some line of work where he can discover big gamblers. If the junketmaster works full time at it, he always has contacts where the big gamblers congregate (bars, restaurants, race tracks, country clubs, etc.). Somebody knows you and they recommend you . . . that's the best way.

The advantages of free transportation and RFB are obvious. The disadvantages are that you are instantly known and kept track of, to make sure you're a gambler and not a freeloader. And, if you're looking for the full Class-A treatment, you should be prepared to play at a fairly high level ($25 chips).

When you're ready to declare yourself, and can meet the conditions, it's a very nice way to go. Very.

---

all, you should have been out making money before you ever got to this chapter . . . right? I just wouldn't have felt right if you didn't have the information to be able to push the Expert System to the outer limits, should you be so inclined. And some of this stuff—like adjusting for Aces—is a bear if you attempt it when you're first starting out.

So relax, move on, and enjoy.

There is great skill in knowing how to conceal one's skill.

Francois, Duc de la Rochefoucauld

He that wrestles with us strengthens our nerves and sharpens our skill. Our antagonist is our helper.

Edmund Burke

A good reputation is more valuable than money.

Publilius Syrus

Win without boasting. Lose without excuse.

Albert Payson Terhune

The good old rule
Sufficeth them, the simple plan,
That they should take,
Who have the power,
And they should keep who can.

William Wordsworth

6 The Experts' Guide to Keeping Your Name on the Welcome Mat

Being a diverse discussion of such
sundry topics as The Future of the
Game, Cheating, Getting Barred and
a discourse on maneuvering
through the world of Blackjack
System Play by the Experts themselves

Glance at the chapter descriptions above and take a deep breath —you're about to get the inside track on a great number of subjects of vital interest to any serious Blackjack player. This time, my contributors aren't getting the opening words because I think this general information needs to be put in perspective first. Then you'll get some very inside goodies directly from the mouths of those experts, describing how they see things as professionals who beat Blackjack from the outside. And also—where pertinent— you'll get my comments as to how the game looks from the inside.

Despite the wealth of varied information assembled here, it wouldn't surprise me if most people who read this book skipped to this chapter in order to get detailed answers to just two questions: 1) How long can I play—or how much money can I make—before I'm detected and barred? and 2) How long will it be before I get cheated out of my bankroll? Those are the two questions most people interested in Blackjack have asked me around the country when they find I'm a pit boss out of Vegas.

Well, you can appreciate how many people become intrigued with these questions when you remember how much sensational material comes out on those subjects through newspapers, magazines and TV.

Dress Codes

They're not written, but they exist in gambling circles just as they do everywhere.

Take a look around. People on the Vegas Strip dress a little nicer, maybe a little flashier, than in most other places. People at Tahoe dress a little better than the shirtsleeves set in downtown Reno or Vegas. Some foreign casinos require ties; most people wear more formal clothes.

As a player, it's good to blend in with the natives at whatever level you're betting and wherever you happen to be.

It's probably a bad idea to walk into a $50 million casino, look for a place to put your backpack, and pull out a bankroll of $4.50.

On the other hand, if it requires a backpack to haul your bankroll. . . .

Further, all those system pushers keep things stirred up by claiming they were barred because their systems are so powerful. Powerful, indeed! Try and find one of them who will look you in the eye and claim he made a fraction of the money playing 21 as he has selling to others what didn't work for him. And as for the sensation about cheating, don't most of the current Blackjack authors claim they have been cheated repeatedly?

Amateurs!

Granted, they might know a great deal about math, merchandising or merrymaking, but they know very little about consistently making money playing Blackjack. Don't listen to the amateurs with their self-destructing systems.

In order to make sure *you* don't fall prey to the general paranoia that engulfs the area of system play at Blackjack, this chapter supplies you not only with the answers to the cheating and barring questions, but provides you with information to stem the tide of a flood of other questions you might have as well.

But before we get to the answers, let *me* ask just one question. If you were selling a system "theoretically" capable of making hundreds of thousands of dollars, how could you convince anyone you would part with it for a few bucks?

To Be Or Not To Be

In case you missed it in the text, here's the guy not to model yourself after: The Typical Card-Counting System Player.

Here's what he looks like: He is grim, glum, tense, intense, furtive, calculating, and guilty-looking. He looks like he has just done something terrible and is expecting the firing squad. He also avoids eye contact, bets very carefully, plays too long, quickly adds money to his bet at the last second, and is some-what hyped-up . . . laughing too robustly or frowning too hard. He never sits down until he has circled the tables a few times and inspected all the help closely.

If he is a Publicity-Seeking Card-Counting System Seller, he does all this in the company of two other people: a publicity agent and a lawyer.

Yup. Tell the yokels that every pit boss and dealer on every shift of every casino in the entire state of Nevada and in the entire world trembles with fear when you walk through the door. And now that all of the inside personnel—each and every last one—has barred you so you can't make money with this wonderful system, you might just as well pass it on. Doesn't being barred—or even cheated, for that matter—prove system power?

The lengths some Blackjack system pushers have gone to get barred to publicize their books might startle you. If you're in the mood for getting startled, send for our *Special Report on Blackjack Systems* (details in chapter 7) for many more specifics than we can justify space for here.

But much more important than the dirty tricks some of these pushers use as selling techniques is the question of real power in systems. Our Special Report will tell you exactly where the power is, down to the last decimal point. *All* current popular systems are analyzed mathematically, their counting procedures named, num-bered and analyzed, and their overall effectiveness discussed from both mathematical and practical points of view. Read it and see for yourself where the power and practicality is.

So much for now on paranoia generated by the press and by

system sellers getting barred. But, you ask, isn't getting barred a problem? Of course. But not as great a problem as you've been led to believe. And cheating? Again, a possible problem, but not anywhere near as great as you've been led to believe.

You'll get detailed answers to these and perhaps countless other questions as you read on, but you'll also get something much more valuable: perspective, so you can make your own judgments. Best of all, you'll learn how to maneuver around most possible difficulties the way the experts do . . . and from the Experts themselves. Hang in there; it's an exciting trip, and this kind of inside information is not available anywhere else.

Now to the perspective I promised, a balanced overview of the game of Blackjack under present conditions. In order to present some accurate insights, I will attempt to answer the toughest questions people have asked me upon discovering I was considering working on a Blackjack book.

How can Blackjack survive if you're going to give a simple and legitimate way of consistently winning at it? Won't the casinos pull the welcome mat for everyone?

Believe that Blackjack will be around for a long, long time, and for the very good reason we mentioned before: profit reports. Imagine you're a casino owner as you look at these figures; bear in mind that 1963 was the first year *after* Thorp published "Beat the Dealer," the first popular book to tell how to beat 21.

Percentage Increase in the Number
of Casino Games in Nevada

% Increase in the Total Number of Casino Games
(Excluding 21) from 1963–76 .... 54%
% Increase in the Total Number of Blackjack Games
Only from 1963–76 .... 171%

The percentage increase in the number of 21 games was more than three times greater than the percentage increase in all other games combined!

Now let's take a look at gross profit. Ever since Thorp, Blackjack began increasing drastically in popularity. The year 1972 was

---

Specificity

Being too specific when printing information about Blackjack games is a big problem. If we should say that such and such a shift at such and such a place is a soft touch, it wouldn't be by the time the ink dried.

Beware of authorities who claim to print detailed information on specific casinos, shifts, casino personnel, playing conditions at a certain place, etc. That kind of printed information is too easily tapped by casino personnel, who then begin taking precautions.

With the Expert System, you don't have that problem. If you follow the system, the betting and the playing techniques . . . and maybe you read a little between the lines . . . you're very unlikely to run into difficulty.

After all, most other systems need a big edge to work: a casino where you can get down a 1 to 20 betting spread, a casino manager who never heard of the count, etc.

With the Expert System, you're playing the simplest and most powerful system ever published. Plus, the Experts themselves tell you how to really get it on. Altogether, you can play and make excellent money anywhere with this information. You don't need to know where there's a dealer with only one eye to go against, or any other such nonsense.

Let the others chase their rumored rainbows. If you pay attention, you'll see a real one just about everywhere.

---

the last one in which craps, the former customer favorite, exceeded Blackjack as the leading casino profit maker. By 1974, the gross revenue from 21 exceeded the gross revenue from craps by $48,924,000, or by 20%.

During the 1972–74 period, the gross revenue from craps increased by $45,102,000, or 23%.

During the same 1972–74 period, gross revenue from Blackjack alone increased by $101,515,000, or 54%!

From then on, it has been up, up and away for Blackjack. Now get ready for this one: In 1976, the total gross for Blackjack approached *400 million* dollars.

With that kind of money involved, and that kind of percentage-growth increase, would a casino owner quit offering the game simply because some knowledgeable outside people were getting a little too? The game will survive this book just as it has survived others which told how to beat the game, and for many other reasons I'll specify later.

You mean there have been a lot of people beating the game all along?

Yes, but the systems they used began being unprofitable as casinos got wise and changed conditions—quicker shuffle points, multiple decks, rules, etc. The difference between those first systems and the Expert and Master Systems is that ours are practical in live play, ours locate virtually all favorable situations from the top of the deck, and that ours have playing strategies which are superior in power. Further, you can adjust quickly with the Expert and Master Systems so that rule changes and conditions don't have nearly the disastrous effect they have on other systems (see chapter 5).

So the other systems can't make money?

No, many of them can still make money . . . it's a question of how much, how soon. Under modern, tougher conditions, most systems need a greater betting spread than ours to yield a reasonable profit in a given period of time.

Give me an example.

Say you have a deck which turns favorable early and you're using an adapted 10-count system. That system might locate three situations which indicate a larger than minimum bet; the Expert System might locate five situations, and the Master System turn up six or seven. The way that translates, you have to make bigger bets in fewer situations located with less powerful systems to make the same money as with our more powerful systems.

So what's the big difference. Why is increasing bet size so bad?

Big increases require a much greater bankroll to sustain any reasonable win rate because of the natural function of fluctuation. And big increases make it obvious you're keeping track of cards, since the increases almost always come after a *bunch* of little cards come out; that is, with a weak system.

And big increases get you barred?

Not really. Soon as a dealer sees you jump your bet a bunch every time little cards come out, he knows you're counting and he

---

Book Review: Beat the Dealer

Edward Oakley Thorp was the first writer to publish a winning 21 strategy. His revised edition of Beat the Dealer (1966) still enjoys a brisk sale and deservedly so. It's the best theoretical job any outsider looking in has ever done.

The book still has much to offer, especially for gaining insight into theory and background. It's also interesting to discover that just about everyone has pirated Thorp's work in coming up with systems for sale.

Recommended reading.

---

starts shuffling. Now the deck starts over, with the edge a little against you, and you take your chances.

That's all? Are you saying no one gets barred any more?

No, but it takes some doing to get barred permanently from a Nevada casino. Known felons are prohibited by law from hanging around the clubs. Various criminal and hustler types are either asked to leave or made to feel very uncomfortable. Anyone who creates a big disturbance is asked to leave; if it's a serious disturbance, barred.

Okay, but are you saying the casinos are reluctant to bar Blackjack system players?

Most are definitely reluctant, especially the bigger casinos. In the old days when only hustlers had systems capable of beating Blackjack, it was relatively easy to bar them as unsavory characters. Since Thorp, legitimate people have attempted counting and the casinos have discovered they just can't indiscriminately bar anyone. Right now several court cases are pending which will decide the issue of whether or not legitimate system users can be barred.

What is the economic future of 21 if the courts decide no one can be barred for system play? Won't the games go broke?

No, the future is bright. Casinos aren't going to give up hundreds of millions of dollars just because they can't bar a few

---

Heavenly Game

The scene is heaven and many great Blackjack authorities from centuries past have been resurrected to help a Poor Soul from Iowa make a particularly difficult decision.

All the cards are being played face-up, in the interest of heavenly fairness. The Poor Soul has eleven and he doesn't know whether to double down or not. Gabriel, the dealer, has shown everyone he has a 10 in the hole to go with his upcard 8, for a total of 18. The only remaining card in the deck is a 10, which is known by all, but the Poor Soul also figures he has too much money bet to take chances–three razzbuckniks, a large sum in Iowa.

Grinder: I'd double, but only if you want to maximize your potential.

Thrope: Wait a minute! He lost the three previous hands; there might be cheating going on here. Contact the media!

Brown: Cheating is the reason people don't reach their mathematical expectation. But if you want to know what to do, I'll run a program for you for a small fee.

Modest: I like the way you two guys think; would you mind endorsing my book? As for the decision, if you tipped the dealer in the first few minutes of play, he might not cheat you.

Will's Son: Thrope is right! Thrope is right! Look out for the Kentucky two-step!

Sam Houston: Wait until I get my flash cards. Do I get on a talk show if I get the right answer?

Bowman: I would call that a very, very good deck and I would double in that situation and expect to win 100% of the time.

(Continued)

---

people. There are ways around barring, anyway. The game will be played just about the way it is now with the same procedures in effect that have knocked out all but a handful of skilled players.

The casinos won't change the rules too much, or make the game much tougher, because they already failed at that during the big Thorp scare of 1964. The changes instituted then lasted about two weeks, drove most of the regular customers away and didn't even slow down good system players (chapter 5 gives details).

Don't forget, most people are already system players—their

Heavenly Game (Cont.)

Paul Revere: *You are not absolutely accurate in that decision. There is a small chance the dealer could have a heart attack, drop the cards and there would be a reshuffle. The accurate odds, therefore, are 99.786429850985 percent in your favor. I would still double, but it's vital to be absolutely accurate in your decisions.*

　　Iam: *(Looking the dealer in the eye for tell-tale signs) What would you do in this spot, Gabriel?*

　　Goodbar: *Is this the new 21 or the old 21?*

　　Hungry: *Will they still comp him into the gourmet room if he gets too far ahead?*

　　Scarme: *I don't like to let out too much inside information, but for a consulting fee of . . . Would you like me to do a card trick while we're waiting?*

　　Party: *That fries me. The Poor Soul ought to have a much bigger betting spread.*

　　Robwarts: *He'd know how to play, have a place to stay, and have a lot of free slot machine coupons if he ordered my book.*

　　Author: *Sure, I used to work on the Strip, but you don't seriously think this game can be beaten from the outside? Would you mind if I played a little after the shuffle?*

　　Mrs. Ms.: *Are you letting me have the last word because you think women always want the last word? Double.*

　　The Poor Soul, *who never listened to anyone in his life or after, Surrendered, took back half his money and left. "Better to have half of three razzbuckniks without risk–that's a lot of money in Iowa," he explained.*

systems just don't happen to work, or they can't work them. Which casino, then, will be first to announce that no one can beat its Blackjack games? The owners are greedy, but not stupid; they know that a small percent taken from the money brought by millions of players is better than 100 percent profit on a game nobody will play.

What casinos will continue to do is make it difficult for the snores with leaky systems to make any money playing. Early shuffle, multiple decks and the like will continue to knock out marginal counters because it will simply be unprofitable for them to play. Known counters might be dealt one hand an hour, and so forth.

But they're not going to slow up the game too much for regular customers. That's where the profit is—the more and the faster hands are dealt, the more money the casino makes. We had an efficiency expert in one time who showed us that if we slowed our games down just five percent in order to take a few more precautions against counters, it would cost us over a million dollars a year in profits! All the bosses got together and calculated we weren't losing $50,000 a year to counters, so the idea of changing things at a cost of one million dollars on the chance of *possibly* saving $50,000 was rejected as absurd.

So you don't think the game will change too much?

No, and for strictly economic reasons. Profits are increasing so that casinos have incentive not to tinker too much with a good thing. Right now, under present conditions, they don't lose a fraction of one percent of profits to the handful of counters still capable of overcoming those conditions. Casinos easily make up any losses successful counters cause from people with unsuccessful systems.

The charm of Blackjack, and what makes it so popular, is that it *theoretically* can be beaten. That keeps the customers flocking in and playing the one game that's "smart" to play. At the exact moment regular customers see no one can beat the game, they'll switch from Blackjack at six to sixteen percent—or more—against them, depending upon how *much* they know about the game, back to craps where they only have 1.4 percent against them on the pass line no matter how *little* they know about the game.

And you don't think publishing the Expert System, and offering the more powerful Master System will hurt the game? Suppose a lot of people use your systems, won't they make Blackjack unprofitable to offer?

I guess it *could* happen, but it won't. I'll give you five good reasons why.

1) Differentiation. How can people make an intelligent choice between the dozen or so systems on the market? All claim to be the greatest. I say, my contributors say, and we can *prove,* the Ex-

---

Book Review: Playing Blackjack as a Business

Lawrence Revere's book first appeared in the middle 1960's and essentially picked up where Thorp left off. It has maintained a steady popular sale and offers substantial basic information, much of it presented through attractive color charts. The book has been revised regularly.

As the title suggests, the book approaches Blackjack as a no-nonsense business. It takes readers from simple to complex systems, and offers more advanced ones through mail order.

All of the Revere systems work, with varying degrees of success. The mail order ones are among the most powerful ever offered generally, about on a par with the Humble systems, though Revere's retain an edge in technique.

Our Special Report on Blackjack Systems has the details on all of the popular strategies currently in use, for those who want to get to the bottom line in comparison.

Revere's book has earned a secure niche in the field of Blackjack literature.

Recommended reading.

---

pert System is superior and the Master System is unequaled in power, ease and in-play performance. Having gained experience in writing this book, I am moving on to other projects. My contributors will sell a limited number of Master Systems and will then no longer be interested in generating more competition for themselves.

Suppose our systems make a big impact? Don't expect those cats who do nothing but sell systems for a living to roll over and play dead. They simply can't do better on the mathematics involved in our systems, nor can they match my contributors' track record in actual play. But they can *say* they did, can, will or might. And they can come with bigger promotion budgets and with persuasive gimmicks and extravagant claims. After all, that *is* their business.

Let me tell you for sure I'm not about to compete in this market forever. Oh, I will absolutely meet my obligations to readers and keep them up to date on systems and the game, but I am not

William's Tell

One of our dealers on another shift presented a particularly difficult mystery for that pit to solve. His table was always full, even when others were empty, and it always lost when he was dealing.

That something was drastically wrong became apparent when a flock of regulars would wait for William to come on shift before they would play, then desist when he went on breaks or got off. All the bosses knew he was scrupulously honest, though his sympathies were always with the customers and he liked to see them win.

Unmistakably, William had a "tell," some subconscious gesture or mannerism he made which helped customers play their hands. The bosses watched for gestures or tell-tale expressions and found none. They listened closely, but only heard conversation. Finally, one of the bosses unknown on that shift managed to get a seat in the game, which by now was the laughing-stock of the casino.

Sure enough, every time William looked at his hole card, if he had a "pat" hand he would make a slight clucking noise with his tongue, kind of like one-half of a "tsk tsk." But when one of the bosses would sidle up, someone at the table would engage him in conversation.

Naturally, they had to tell William not to be so sympathetic, and naturally, he lost his following.

The point is that many dealer's accidentally tip off their hand, if you know what to look for. An old saw is the one about dealer's looking twice at their hole card when they have a 10 up if there's a 4 or other small card underneath: they want to make doubly sure they don't have an Ace there for a Blackjack. That one is so old and tired and well-watched that only break-in dealers make the mistake.

(Continued)

interested in making Blackjack my life's work—I've already stacked up 20 years of work in that field right now. This book is a chance to make my mark, do some good for my readers, and frankly, to have the last laugh at quite a load of hotshot "authorities" who have held an undeserved limelight for too long.

Don't get me wrong. I admire the prodigious effort the system folk put into compilation, correlation and invention. But it's a lot

William's Tell (Cont.)

But other tells do crop up. Sometimes a dealer will give you all the time in the world to make a decision if they have a hand made, then press you for a quick decision if they don't. Sometimes the reverse. Sometimes a dealer will hit you quickly the instant you motion, if he has a hand, but hit you more slowly if he doesn't. Unfortunately, sometimes the reverse.

Each individual dealer is different, and may behave differently with various customers.

Sometimes, though, you can key in on a certain dealer who has a particular tell for certain kinds of situations. When you can, it can help your play enormously. If you "know" a dealer is stiff, for instance, you can stand, double and split as if he had a baby card up.

But you need experience before you can really rely on dealer tells. Often, dealer behavior changes radically when someone starts winning a lot. He feels the bosses might be watching, and perhaps suspect him of cheating or tipping off his play, and he alters all of his patterns so as to be letter-perfect.

That's when you can get in real trouble. Say you wouldn't normally double with a 10 against his upcard 10, but you've read his tell to say he's stiff. Now you double, only to discover he already has a solid hand.

After you can read the subtle nuances of dealer behavior accurately, you'll find that about one in four will help you subconsciously maybe once or twice a play. That's dandy, and a very nice edge to have.

But until you feel confident, be very cautious.

And oh yes, if you do find someone as blatant as William, keep it to yourself and make a good thing last.

like studying to be a great lover. People like Errol Flynn and Cassanova *got it on;* people like Masters and Johnson simply compile a lot of data on the subject. Two different approaches, both valid, depending upon what you want.

The point of all of this is that most people aren't in a position to differentiate between quality of approach or quality of information.

2) Competition. This is beginning to sound like a terrible ego trip, and for that I apologize. But as the system pushers discover where they've gone wrong, they'll revise their material to try and compensate for the innovations my contributors have revealed. They will claim "new and improved," promote heavily, and sell more of their products. That's the nature of competition, and that's very good for you. To give you a conservative estimate, the record of Blackjack systems to date is that for every person capable of playing a good system and winning, there has been at least a thousand playing a poor one and losing.

3) Interest and Motivation. Most folks who buy this book won't be sufficiently interested to really go out and do it, and for many reasons not all peculiar to 21. For instance, how many people do you know who are motivated enough to become expert welders, bakers, accountants, writers, etc.? It's unfortunate, but there isn't much possibility for the semi-skilled to win consistently at Blackjack. And though all the directions are here, not many people will follow them.

There are other things involved. Some capable people aren't physically close enough to gambling to play regularly. Some people can't handle the fluctuation of the short run or can't keep their eyes on the long run. Some can't manage money. Some are too paranoid, or too bold ("You can't ask me not to play, I'm from Detroit and I'll sue . . ."). Some have no patience. Some can't overcome the fascination of gambling. Many give in to short term hunches, ESP, etc. In net effect, most would like to, but won't.

4) Cup of Tea. When you think about it, how many people can you imagine would *want* to beat 21 regularly? The major satisfaction is getting the money, and most people need the additional satisfaction of the approval of others (no one stands up and cheers when you make an exceptionally good play). As an extreme example, imagine an entertainer saying, "I think I'll get down from this stage away from all this applause and double my income anonymously." Never happen.

Then there's the known and the unknown. Many people who would otherwise be able to do it will only do so when they exhaust more familiar opportunities. I think a lot of people will keep the possibility of beating Blackjack like a succulent piece of filet

---

Book Review: The Archer Method of Winning at 21

John Archer's book is very practical and probably contains the best techniques written by an outsider to gambling. The book is free of hysteria and razzle-dazzle, and gives a modest system for a modest win.

Interestingly, while the book's recommended system is dated in concept, the techniques for application are nicely reasoned out and surprisingly viable. For that reason, it's a good bet that Archer system players stand to make a higher return than players who have bought mathematically better systems which recommend questionable playing procedures.

Intelligent observation and considered comment make this: Recommended reading.

---

mignon simmering on the back burner—ready to pounce on when they'd like to.

5) Last and Best. The final reason I think writing this book won't damage the game is probably the best: this book will actually *help* the game, though certainly not because of the people who buy it and put the system to work.

It will help because *any* book on the subject generates interest in Blackjack system play. People who win with the Expert System will eventually talk about it. Emphasis in the media will shift from the subject of players getting barred to players winning.

Now the chain reaction. Regular customers will play more, because the idea the game can be beaten will be reinforced. Someone will say their system is better and promote it heavily. More folk will rush into the casinos with new systems and fresh money. The casinos will make even more money, and at the same time scream they are being robbed.

Everyone will be happy.

You're a windy devil; can you summarize your overview briefly?

As of now, more people play Blackjack than any other casino game, thus making it the most popular and profitable game offered. This popularity is a direct result of people believing that the game can be outsmarted. Many try; few succeed.

The Expert and Master Systems enable you to play profitably under current conditions, and both can be adjusted to remain lucrative should conditions and rules change. There is not likely to be enough Expert System players to counterbalance the legions of customers who lose, with and without systems. It is to my contributors' best interest to never release enough Master Systems to hurt the game.

With either the Expert or the Master System you play just about like a regular customer. You can even make money with no bet variation in many games. By following the tips in this book to disguise play, and considering built-in adjustments to thwart casino rule changes or varying conditions, the Expert or Master system player who exercises reasonable judgment can make a great deal of money.

The rest of this chapter reveals how my contributors—the Experts themselves—think and conduct themselves as they go about consistently winning at 21, and how they avoid the pitfalls of being detected and barred. Don't expect them all to agree on everything; though each must obviously play within mathematical confines called for by system play, each has developed a unique style.

Be prepared for some penetrating insights into the game while you sit in on these round-table discussions. But remember these are general comments; the nitty-gritty mechanics are spelled out in previous chapters.

So here we go. Let me re-introduce my contributors. There's Grinder, who has played about 25 years; Hungry, 20 year's experience; Party, about 10 years; and Mrs. Ms., about five years. You recall that Mrs. Ms. is Grinder's daughter and that she and Party were recently married. As you listen to all their comments about the game, keep in mind they have played successfully for a total of approximately 60 years without any one of them being barred from any casino anywhere in the world. I already mentioned my long career as a pit boss on the Las Vegas Strip. Any time I comment during the following discussions, my remarks follow the identification, "Author."

Pull up a chair and listen now, as the Experts respond to my questions.

Do you worry about cheating when you go out to play Blackjack?

Grinder: Hardly at all. If you confine your play to the bigger, long-established casinos both in Nevada and across the world, there is virtually no chance even an amateur will lose any significant amount of his money to cheating, in the long run.

Hungry: (Laughs) You qualified that to the point I might consider giving up playing.

Grinder: Well, there are few things in the world you can say with 100% certainty. It's really a question of odds and incentive. In Nevada, any given casino has one license to lose which covers all gambling. The odds of risking profits from slot machines, baccarat, craps, etc. for the sake of cheating someone are very remote . . . that would be risking millions to cheat some poor sucker out of —relatively speaking—a few bucks. Not much incentive.

Hungry: That's mostly true. The big stores (casinos) make it on a huge volume, and any individual player can hardly lose enough to make a percentage-point difference in profits.

Party: Well, I started out as a dealer and I can tell you for sure there is cheating. Maybe not so much in the big spots, but. . . .

Mrs. Ms.: By "not so much," do you mean you know of any major casino which cheats as a matter of policy?

Party: None I know of right now. But there's a few little ones, for sure. Right, Hungry?

Hungry: Well, I don't know about right now, but as you know, two years ago when I converted to the Master System from the Expert System I wanted to give it a dry run for small stakes. I played in the smaller Nevada towns, and after logging 30 hours I was about even. I'd say that given my betting spread, and my inexperience with the new system, that put the cheating rate at about four percent.

Mrs. Ms: Did you actually see anyone cheat?

Styles: Party

Back when I used to deal the game, I noticed the bosses smiled the broadest when someone would come in and "throw a party."

It's a style of play instantly recognizable to most insiders, and guaranteed to make them happy if they own some stock.

People who throw a party in a casino make a lot of sudden action, usually find the wrong bets to make, and almost always lose.

It sounds screwy, but at some point in their play they are often a ton ahead, yet they're a cinch to keep jamming it out there until they lose.

Whoopeeee!

When everyone started getting paranoid about counting, I remembered the people who threw parties.

I remembered a particular cat who came in with a $20 bill and got out (won) about $4,000.

"You think that guy knows something?" I said to the boss; "he bets $5 three times in a row, then he bets $200."

The boss laughed. "He knows one thing," he said. "He's supposed to throw all his money right straight in the air, and whatever stays up is his to keep."

Sure enough, the guy loses it all back in the next 20 minutes. He stamps and hollers and then . . . fishes up another $20 bill. His last, he announces slyly.

Sure as Shinola, he now runs that one up to $3,000 before he takes a bath (loses the whole thing).

Yahooooo!

That's the way I like to play, quitting winners, of course. Only no

(Continued)

Hungry: Definitely at one spot, which has since folded. But the rest of it—if there was any—went over my head.

Grinder: That's the problem with cheating. A really good mechanic (cheating dealer) doesn't have to cheat very often or very obviously to get your money. That's why the best hedge is playing where you're least likely to be cheated.

Hungry: Well, it's really not very bright to play in a tiny casino where they can't afford to lose, anyway. When a spot has plenty of

---

Styles: Party (Cont.)

one, absolutely no human, is going to get down a betting spread of from $5 to $200 consistently these days.

So I modify the whole thing, with the same idea.

Maybe I walk up to a table with my wallet in my hand and flop a $5 bill on the layout. I lose and it's plus. I drop a $100 bill and I look mad—I'm steaming . . . chasing losing bets. I keep doing that as long as the deck is plus. When it goes minus, my wallet is suddenly empty and I have to cash a check.

The idea is that as long as the deck is plus, and I have the money out there, the system is going to come through.

Or maybe I throw a big party with $5 chips; bad decisions, big jumps in the betting spread. They've got me pegged and maybe they don't notice so much when I play a smaller spread with $25 chips and make better decisions.

Or say I just condition them to shoving my money out in stacks at all the wrong times and gradually work into only the right times.

There's a million ways to look erratic, jerky and seem like a goof-off. A million ways to throw a party.

Well, that's my favorite style, but I had to quit it. That was best when I could get a pile, lay back and let everyone forget me. Maybe that might be best for occasional players, though you need to back yourself with a big enough bankroll to handle the fluctuation.

Since I got married I settled into a routine that's less sensational. I probably make more now just because I stay in the background and can play in one spot longer. Me and Mrs. Ms. are keeping a quieter, steadier pace now.

Sure was fun, though, that Party bit.

---

action, they really don't have to cheat to make it. The economics are such, that a casino stands to lose much more in the long run by cheating. For instance, when any store begins running flat (cheating), word gets out and business falls off.

Grinder: It's a pretty difficult thing to keep quiet for long. A dealer or dealers have to do the dirty work; usually a pit boss has to be in on it and maybe a casino manager. Then the eye in the sky (security behind two-way mirrors) has to look the other way.

All these people tend to talk, or live beyond their salaries or at least warn relatives and friends not to play in that casino. So word gets out. And don't forget, to make it *worthwhile* requires making a lot of moves. While not everyone watching the games is an investigator from the Gaming Commission looking to board the place up for cheating, not everyone is a sucker, either. Many hustlers who know all the moves watch and gamble, too; if *they* get cheated, they have to be bought off at best. In any case, no casino can survive if enough people scream.

Party: Then there's the problem of chopping up the money. Anyone who knows—or strongly suspects—what's going on gets a piece of the action, if just to keep their face shut. Pretty soon everyone is in and everyone is moving.

Grinder: Of course the biggest problem of cheating is who cheats who. If a boss hires someone capable of cheating a customer for a thousand or two, that someone is liable to have better moves for cheating the casino out of hundreds of thousands. If a dealer is capable of giving you bad hands, he can give an accomplice good hands. That's why the big casinos don't want any cheating of any kind against anyone. To make sure, they install TV cameras, two-way mirrors, floating security, pit bosses . . . dozens of safeguards.

Hungry: In the end, cheating from either the inside or the outside gets directed against the casino bankroll. *That's* worth shooting for.

Party: You might add that at times *outside* cheaters give counters a bad reputation. Maybe a crew of desperados comes in and switches decks, or marks the cards or holds out, and the loss sometimes gets blamed on Blackjack counters. That's a joke.

Author: An even bigger joke is that many techniques casinos have tried to stop counters have ended up *costing* them a great deal of money. For instance, when a dealer picks up cards face down so potential counters can't see them, the casino leaves itself open to lose more in one night due to the danger of that move alone than it could lose to counters in a year.

What it all boils down to is that for one reason or another, it's to a casino's long-range best interests not to cheat. Anything you'd care to add to that?

Book Review: The Casino Gambler's Guide

Allan Wilson's 1970 (revised) book has much to recommend it. It deals with much more than Blackjack, and most of the subjects are treated thoroughly and well. Nice reading for insight into many areas of interest, as perceived by a solid mathematician who has a popular style.

The playing system the book recommends is workable and winning, but weak.

Very good reading for background.

Grinder: Sure: If there was any significant cheating going on in the big casinos, how could all of us win consistently for all these years. Further, given any segment of 100 hours of play, we're all within the tiniest fraction of where we're supposed to be, both in percentage and dollar win.

Party: That doesn't mean you don't take precautions, though. Like play in the big places and don't play against any dealer who always wins . . . maybe he's moving money off to a friend and is doing a little free-lance cheating to cover it.

Hungry: Some good books describe many common cheating moves . . . Scarne's *New Complete Guide to Gambling* and Garcia's *Marked Cards and Loaded Dice* are both fairly good. Knowing the most common moves gives you confidence. I ought to add, though, that worrying about cheating isn't worth the effort as a general rule. Years ago, Grinder and I hired a succession of card manipulators—you'd recognize some of their names—and also card hustlers, to show us everything we could possibly have to worry about when playing 21. In the past five years, neither Grinder nor I have found anyone in the big stores doing anything to speak of.

Grinder: To be sure, a good trick is to never lose more than one fifth of a Playing Bankroll (see "Money Management," chapter 4) against any one dealer, and don't go back against a dealer you've lost to three times in a year.

Mostly, I think cheating is overrated as a threat. Amateurs and the system hawkers use that as an excuse for losing in the short run. Most people think of cheating first, when they should be thinking about fluctuation and expectation.

Take a statistical example: say you have $100 bet in a very favorable situation where you have a ten percent advantage. That's a dynamite situation, but it really means your expectation is $10 on that $100 bet. Now, say you get in that betting situation 100 times in the next year . . . your expectation is a $1,000 profit on a total of $10,000 bet. The way you will get the $1,000 is to win 55 out of the 100 hands, but lose 45 of them. Now, of the 45 losers, it wouldn't be enormously unusual to lose three, or four, or maybe even eight or nine in a row, though in the long run you'll make $1,000 because of the 55 winners.

Soon as the amateurs—and that includes mathematicians and other so-called smart folk with systems—*lose* a few bets where they figure they have the best of it, they would like to believe they've been cheated. They really just don't understand normal expectation and fluctuation. (See appendix—author.)

On the other hand, maybe some of those people who claimed they were cheated *were* cheated. I guess all we can really say is that we're all confident we're not being cheated in any major casino. I find it hard to understand why a casino wouldn't try to cheat Hungry or me when we're playing $500 and $1,000 a hand, but *would* attempt to cheat some smart system player risking a whole $5 a hand . . . but I guess it could happen.

Party: I can imagine one way some snore might get himself cheated. See, when you guys bet $500 and up a smash, no one ever suspects you're counting. But say some guy waltzes up to a table and says, "I'm playing a rootee-toot system and I'm going to take all your money and make you guys look silly, and there's not a blasted thing you can do about it—you have to sit still for it even if it costs you your jobs; so take that, jerks!"

I don't know what casino personnel would do in that case, but I know that's a very big threat to take sitting still. I know *I* would bar the guy, or cheat him, or spill a drink in his lap, or *something* to distract him if I was in that spot.

Hungry: I don't think I'd want to *defy* anyone to stop *my* play. That's just unprofessional. Winning at Blackjack is simply not an adversary proceeding—better to have them all laughing and loving you as you cart off their money. You're just playing for fun; the money doesn't count. And you can't be jolly and have fun if you're making enemies right and left. The objective is to get the money, not glory, or enemies, or hard feelings, or resentment.

Author: Let's try a quick summary. You all agree, that to your knowledge, there is no cheating in major casinos as a matter of policy. If there is, it is isolated and rare and usually by individual employees trying to steal; even in that case, the cheating is more likely to be directed against the house. You wouldn't ever declare yourselves and challenge anyone to try and stop you.

However, because there is always the *possibility,* you all take reasonable precautions. You've read the books and tried to learn as much as you could. You play in bigger casinos where the incentive is to be scrupulously honest. You limit your losses against a single dealer. That's in addition to the sound money management principle of limiting your losses on a single play (see chapter 4). Overall, you believe there is little cheating because it is economically sounder for the casinos not to, and that the Gaming Commission provides a reasonable deterrent, besides the threat of general discovery.

Grinder: Well, it sounds cynical, but that's true. I think you have more chance of being cheated at a car agency than a major Nevada casino, or for that matter, a major casino anywhere in the world. It's a good idea to be aware of what *could* happen; it's a very bad idea to worry about what is very unlikely to happen if you take normal precautions. How do you see it, Pit Boss; do *you* think we should worry more?

Author: As you know, I've worked in the biggest operations in the state and to my best knowledge cheating has never been a house policy. That doesn't mean no one ever cheated anyone where I've worked; it just means everything we could possibly do to prevent *anyone* from cheating was done. Putting the clamp on cheating has to be absolute; selective cheating just isn't possible— the house gets taken eventually. That's probably why all the insiders I know won't tolerate cheating . . . though some might like to. It always eventually backfires.

Grinder: I'd have to say that I can't find it in my heart to believe all these big casinos are imbued with integrity—but I would have to agree that something is keeping them straight. I know I'm about a dollar and a half of where I'm supposed to be with return on the Master System for the years I've kept track. Now, I get about $50,000 an hour minimum in action—if they cheated, why wouldn't they take dead aim at me?

Okay. Let's call it quits on cheating. Now, how much consideration should a newcomer give to being barred?

Grinder: Plenty, because that's the worst thing a casino can do to you—decline your action. It's easy to avoid, if you model yourself after the average customer. No one hassles the average Joe, because that's where the house makes money. And don't forget; a lot of average guys have systems, almost all losers when played long enough.

Hungry: You have to remember that casino personnel are reluctant to take extreme action against anyone unless they're absolutely sure that person can *consistently* beat them. Even then, they'd rather take lesser measures, like shuffling early when you make your big bet, or providing the distraction of having a pit boss at your shoulder constantly, or generally making you feel unwelcome or uncomfortable. It's not like the old days when only hustlers had potentially winning systems and could be intimidated. Now that *reputable* citizens are playing systems, casinos are likely to get sued if they abuse people.

Party: Yeah, maybe they can sue for bad treatment or getting hassled, but let's take a long shot and suppose the courts go along and eventually prohibit casinos from barring system players. Is anyone stupid enough to think he could march into a major casino and announce he's going to own the place—and expect them to deal until he does?

Grinder: The way you get barred is to either be a system seller looking for publicity, or to play a system which is so weak it forces you to play in a way which tips off the fact you're a counter.

Mrs. Ms.: Not necessarily. You can tip off any system if you study the cards too intently as they come out, take too much time to make decisions, or bet too obviously.

Grinder: Aside from the possibility of greed, I like to think of

---

Asked to Leave, as Opposed to Being Barred

You should never be asked to leave or told to refrain from playing after you have read this book. If it does happen, there is something wrong with your play. Usually a casino will employ such obvious countermeasures before asking you to leave (see text), that you can easily throw them off. If asked to leave, don't stand around and argue.

Should you be asked to leave a particular establishment, you will find you can come back within a week or so and play on another shift, if you've handled the situation quietly and intelligently.

If the courts decide no one can be barred or asked to leave for playing a system, you will still make more money playing unobtrusively (see text) than by attempting to enforce your "rights."

---

those tip-offs as related to the strength of your system and how well you play it. If you play a system too complex for you, you have to study and stare and stall to make the right mental computations. As for greed, theoretically you can make more in the long run if you bet a bunch when you have the edge. But in practice, you make much more if your betting schedule doesn't put everyone on guard.

Party: Yeah, that's the big tip-off. A guy bets one unit, one unit, one unit; then out come a bunch of little cards and here comes a big bet. A guy who bets like that isn't going to make any money playing—he's going to have to make his money suing the casinos after they bar him.

Grinder: So you bet like the average guy. Now, maybe someone who wants to win a lot of money suddenly will vary his betting greatly, but the average guy doesn't—win or lose, he wants to last a while and play. Maybe he's afraid to bet too much for fear he might lose, or bet too little for fear he might win. In any case, he stays within reasonable limits between high and low bets.

Hungry: That's usually right. The average player may plunge a bit once in awhile, but it isn't always just after the little cards come out.

Styles: Grinder

It may sound strange, but having a powerful system is only part of the battle when you play for big stakes. The people inside respect money in large amounts, they know that any given play can go either way, and they want to feel secure that any steady big player is a bonafide, certified loser in the long haul.

That's because the so-called gamblers on the inside are really businessmen. As businessmen they want a profit, even though they've been trapped into offering a game which some people can beat. Experience should tell you that no one likes to be beaten at his own game, whether it's in real estate, manufacturing, checkers, auto sales, architecture or Blackjack.

This you can bank on: the guy who is likely to like you the least is the guy you beat at the game he thinks he knows best. Paste that in your hat.

At the lower levels in Blackjack play, say $25 and under in a major casino, it's not so critical. A few throw-offs, as described in the text, and you're home free. But when any single player starts accounting for dollar movement at levels that involve three, four and five figures, someone is going to get curious. The businessmen want to know they have a chance, too, and that the money isn't always going to go (to them) the wrong way.

Give 'em a security blanket, when you get to the higher levels. Let them pigeonhole you in their minds as an ultimate loser. They'll feel secure and they'll love you for it.

Call it style. There's an infinite number you can assume, but pick one that fits your basic nature and personality and with

(Continued)

Grinder: What you need to look absolutely average is a very powerful system which locates as many betting situations as possible. This allows you to make frequent medium-sized bets for a reasonable profit. To make the same money with a weak system, you have to make very large bets when the system finally gets around to locating favorable situations.

Hungry: You have to use judgment with any system. It's a good idea to experiment cautiously until you get an idea what they'll sit still for, and what they won't.

Styles: Grinder (Cont.)

which you can play within the necessary mathematical confines.

Because I've been playing a long time, and because of the way I started out, I evolved a very simple style. I'm actually known as a "tough" player, one who knows a goodly amount about the game.

But upon close scrutiny, they find that I make enough gross "mistakes" and "bad plays" to insure that in the long run I am going to lose. In the end, they decide, they are going to grind me down. And sure enough, at the end of a three or four day stay, most of the time I do appear to lose . . . on paper. Their judgment is confirmed, and I leave kidding that they'd better watch out for next time.

The way I appear to make mistakes and bad plays might not be what you think: I almost never purposely make a wrong decision simply to throw someone off. I'm much more direct. Quite simply, I play the best system in the world today (the Master System), and I play it as accurately as possible each and every hand. My decisions, and the decisions of someone checking me out, inevitably diverge. Enough insiders agree, someone hits my forehead with the rubber stamp which says "loser," and I'm home free. Note, though, that I never tempt the fates too much by trying to get too big a betting spread down. That's the biggest thing they look for.

That's about if for me, straight ahead. They would love me more if I made terrible plays every time, but they're content knowing that I make enough bad ones to have erosion, attrition and the "odds" finally grind me down.

Grinder: It's a game of cat-and-mouse. Make a big bet and the dealer shuffles. If you're paranoid, you probably think he's on to you. If you're thinking, you might notice you made the bet at the point he shuffles anyway. Or he might be testing *you* to see if you pull the money back. So you make another big bet when the deck is *unfavorable*. Does he shuffle? If he doesn't, could he possibly be on to you? Now, you don't play too many games like that because they can cost money; but with a powerful system you can afford to do a little testing without losing very much.

Hungry: The screwiest notion is that anyone gets barred with no warning. That's extraordinary. Because they like to be sure, casino personnel almost always telegraph their punches. First you find the dealer shuffling sooner; then maybe a pit boss keeps hanging around; then you start getting anxious glances. Maybe the cocktail girl skips you when asking around for free drinks. Someone makes a rude comment. Maybe someone asks you if you're playing a system, or a pit boss calls over another, whispers and nods in your direction.

It keeps going like that, and if you ignore it, finally someone will suggest you play another kind of casino game. If you ignore that, someone will tell you they'd prefer it if you didn't play Blackjack. If you ignore that, they'll ask you not to play. Ignore that and the dealer stops dealing to you while someone tells you how great a favor it would be if you went someplace else and took all *their* money.

Now, if at any time you raise a big disturbance and disrupt the game and make it difficult for other players to play, you will very likely be asked to leave.

Not all those steps are there all the time, but nowadays at least some of them will be there in any major casino.

Party: The trick is to pull up, or throw them off before anyone gets certain you're a crackerjack player. Make a wrong bet or two, and how sure can they be?

Grinder: I know you like those throw-off bets, Party, but I never give them anything the best of it if I can help it. I will go to betting flat (no bet variation at all) however, and with the Master System I can grind out two or three $100 chips an hour, or at worst, stay even. How can you look any more average than that, betting the same amount every time?

Mrs. Ms.: (Laughs) The average player doesn't bet $100 chips, much less have the Master System.

Party: Well, I haven't converted from the Expert System yet (the one in this book—author), but when I do, I'm going to try for the biggest betting spread I can get. But I guess it's always nice to be able to fall back onto bulletproof play; right, Pit Boss?

Author: It's true that holding down the betting spread is important. But a newcomer also has to make sure he doesn't give himself

---

Book Review: Scarne's New Complete Guide to Gambling

This book is John Scarne's latest and most comprehensive. It's virtually encyclopedic in scope and nicely written. It covers the most popular casino games, plus has information on race and sports betting, carnival games, gin rummy, poker, proposition bets, backgammon, percentage breakdowns, etc.

It's an excellent book for laymen who wish to acquire a broad general knowledge about gambling, as well as some enlightening specifics. Oddly, the book offers sparse information about winning Blackjack play.

Highly recommended, general reading.

---

away by staring at other people's cards as if his life depended on it, or in any other way appearing too intense or too deep in concentration.

Also, believe it or not, most people look *guilty* when they're trying out a system, win or lose. Some stare at the pit bosses all the time. Others look furtive when they make a larger bet. There's lots of little things a pit boss looks for that have nothing to do with how good a system is.

Grinder: Well, that's probably true, but you eliminate those obvious signs as you gain confidence. Incidentally, I've always figured about one pit boss in fifty might be able to detect a good counter strictly from watching play. Would you agree?

Author: I've known maybe a hundred or so pit bosses and not one of them could detect a system player who wasn't reckless. You have to remember there isn't much incentive for a pit boss to learn anything more than the barest rudiments of system play. Even if he is capable of doing the mental work, he doesn't have much time to stand around and count down cards as they're played.

The average system player believes the pit boss is only there to catch card counters. But take a look at what's expected of a pit boss at work: He orders drinks; signs drink checks. He keeps track of the money at the tables; orders and signs for table fills. He

How I Handle Counters: Author

There are a lot of people out trying to count and make money, and that's okay with me. I only have one rule: any one can try at any time where I work, provided they don't put me in the middle. It may not strike you as fair, but my bosses insist that I be alert enough not to allow known counters to have a free rein.

The key word is "known." I would add to that those people with the shabby systems who make themselves obvious immediately.

When someone known, or someone who is very obvious, appears on my shift, I quietly call him aside and deliver my set speech:

"You've been recognized as a card counter. I don't personally care about that one way or the other, but if you play on my shift you are going to put me in a very bad position. You're welcome to play any other game, and you're welcome to use all of our facilities. But I'd appreciate it if you wouldn't play Blackjack."

If the guy is a professional, he recognizes and appreciates this approach. It's quiet, and no extra people are made known of his appearance. He also knows I only asked him not to play on my shift, so he has two others plus my days off.

If the guy is trying to become professional, but still feeling his way, he might pick up that I'm sincere and thereby get some information with which to improve. "What tipped you off?" he might say. "Your betting spread is too big," I might comment. Or, "You're following the cards too closely and you're sweating bullets when you look around. The boss told me you looked like you were about to grab a handful of the dealer's chips and run."

If the guy is a rub-a-dub, he won't let you handle the whole thing quietly. This type has to make a big issue of it, which is to neither of our best interests. Here's some examples, all loud:

"Hey! Are you accusing me of something illegal?"

"What do you mean? I'm not doing anything, and you can't prove it."

"Are you saying I'm barred?"

"You guys really don't want to give anyone a fair shake for their money, do you?"

People like this aren't really interested in the money or they'd understand they can't make any unless they're playing, rather than talking. So I go into phase two:

(Continued)

How I Handle Counters: Author (Cont.)

"It's not going to work to your advantage if you attract a lot of attention. You can't make any money while you're talking to me. You still have two shifts to play in this casino, and three shifts everywhere else in town. I'm asking you for a favor, and that is not to play on my shift where you've been recognized."

When the worst happens, it goes like this: "Well, I'm going to play and you can't stop me!"

Phase three: "All right, sir. Play anywhere you like. We will deal to you from a single deck and if at any time you increase your bet I will instruct the dealer to shuffle. If necessary we will shuffle every hand. You force me to pass along these instructions to the bosses, so they understand what's happening, and to the dealers, so they can carry them out. A lot of unnecessary people will then know you and will find it difficult to make money here. I'm sorry."

When things go that far, the situation is terrible. If the guy plays and loses, he claims he was cheated. If he wins, he loudly announces we tried to cheat him of his rights but he outsmarted us.

The odd thing about it, every time things have deteriorated that badly on my shift, the guy in question was not capable of beating the game consistently under any circumstances!

There's a big difference between a "known" counter and a successful counter.

There's one more character I should mention. He plays very obviously until he gets to hear my Phase One speech. Then he goes right into his Phase One speech:

"Are you saying my system is too powerful for you guys and that you are barring me because I would win too much money if you didn't take forceful action to stop me?"

The words aren't always in that order . . . but close. Upon hearing them, I know I am being confronted by that very wily creature: THE SYSTEM SELLER who is looking for publicity. He can't make it with the system, so now he wants me to help him get free advertising. I go through Phase Two and Three just the same, often choking with laughter.

Ah, you say, but what about those players that you spot and no one else spots who are capable of beating the game?

Ah, I say, and say nothing. I'm too busy watching in case I might pick up a gimmick or two for when I play.

handles credit transactions. He settles disputes and answers the phone. He watches dealers to make sure they're doing their jobs; watches players to see if he can spot known troublemakers or hustlers. He should also know enough to watch for such cheating gimmicks as mucking, capping, cold-decking, crimping, bending, nailing, painting, past posting, combination play and a thousand other moves against the house which can cost some *real* money.

If a pit boss does all these things efficiently, who would expect him to neglect those duties and stand around counting down deck after deck to make sure somebody wasn't making a big bet with an advantage? And suppose a player did, does that prove anything?

So the pit boss looks for irrational betting, furtiveness, intenseness, and then makes a judgment. Given the capability of most systems and most system players, you can guess how often the pit bosses' judgments are wrong. I'd say more than half of all players who have been asked not to play Blackjack because of system play were not capable of beating the game.

Now, if you want to assume the other half had theoretically sound systems, I'd say at least 90% of them couldn't make their systems work *in action*.

Still, pit bosses are very paranoid about counters and feel obligated to "catch" one on a fairly regular basis to let the bosses know they're doing their job.

Grinder: Well, don't knock it; whatever they're doing, it works. The safeguards the casinos have built into the game have a way of catching up and eventually forcing out weak system players.

Author: Good point . . . casinos have become a lot more cautious since Thorp and the others, and take many measures to protect themselves. That leads me to my last question:

Would you be willing to share with newcomers some of the finer points of how you think about the game-as well as play it–under modern conditions?

Grinder: Well, you should keep in mind that almost everyone inside has become a believer—they know the game can be beaten. If you do the gross kinds of things they expect of counters, they're likely to think you're trying to get it on. So you play around their expectations.

Book Review: Your Best Bet

Mike Goodman is a pit boss who has held a number of top jobs in a variety of casinos. His book is loaded with interesting stories, anecdotes and commentary.

The book offers no consistently-winning systems, though some of the betting and playing techniques provide reasonable bankroll protection while preserving a chance for big wins.

There's a lot of captivating material here. You'll be especially interested in the comments on many foreign casinos if you plan to travel.

Party: Like keeping a low profile. What they expect is that a guy who really can beat them will stick around and get all he can. So you spread your action around to different clubs, take a little, leave a little.

Hungry: That's an especially good point for newcomers. Obviously, casino personnel tend to watch people who play regularly and win regularly.

Grinder: You really have the best of it when you're a new face. As you get to be known, you simply have to play cagier. When you start playing $100 checks, you really get known in a hurry and it's impossible to be anonymous, right Pit Boss?

Author: Sure, but it shouldn't be unexpected. Look at it from the casino's point of view. A customer starts playing big chips and wins ten or twenty thousand and *someone* upstairs wants to know who he was and that there was no razzle-dazzle. Win or lose, it's management's advantage to know the guy and his story, if only to cater to him. They'd like him to come back with more action later on. If he's a good and known player, he's probably RFB—gets complimentary room, food and beverages.

Hungry: And is *that* ever sweet. But with that, you *must* play cagey or you don't get invited back. Also, word goes from casino to casino. You want the word to be that you throw your money away in gobs while you're having a good time.

Mrs. Ms.: You might mention that you need a nice-sized bankroll to do the high-roller bit; and also a good cover story.

Styles: Hungry

I try to be the kind of big player casino personnel understand best. Whether or not they know the words, I hope that this is what they see when they look at me:

The money I "lose" is almost incidental. I don't like to lose, but I can afford it. I'm here for a good time, and a good time is being a "big deal". I hope they think it's the ego gratification. Getting recognition. The stroking, the perquisites, the deference. I am hungry to have my needs satisfied. And though I will try to win, I am likely to lose a great deal as long as I am being catered to.

When they see me that way, they can't think of me as too bright. And the store is mine.

Misdirection. I joke and I'm jolly but I like to be called "sir," unless it's by management. I expect a certain amount of surprise, if not sympathy, when I lose because they keep letting me know they figure I could dent them good if my luck changed. And a man who does great battle with the gods of fortune assumes he will be pampered.

They know I want the best, the best of everything. They know I could buy it, but to a man of my stature these things are given. They feed my hungry ego with whatever it seems to need. Blandishments, compliments. They limo my party to the jet and fly us there. They arrange our stay; sightseeing, fishing, golf and, naturally, a "little time for gaming."

That's the end I have to uphold to get the goodies. I know, and they know that I know at a "subconscious" level, that all the "freebies" have to be paid for. But they don't suspect that I know

(Continued)

Grinder: Sure. It takes some money when you know you might get stuck five or ten thousand before you get going. It also helps to have the reputation—or the front—of being a big industrialist from the North, or a playboy who inherited millions, or something to justify the kind of money you "throw around."

Hungry: Also, when you declare yourself like that, you can't play too often in any one spot because eventually, someone is going to wake up to the fact you almost always win a great deal more than you ever lose. Of course, you don't *have* to play as often when you play for higher stakes.

Styles: **Hungry** (Cont.)

that their rule of thumb for courting me is about 25% of the money of my average loss on previous trips, if it's a place where I'm established.

Naturally, I show them a loser on 90% of my trips. I wouldn't like to state exactly how I appear to lose when I'm winning, but the basic methods are simple: when you're taking out markers sometimes, and buying in for cash sometimes, and moving from table to table frequently, and playing a little on three shifts . . . you can see there's a lot of spots where you can hide a buck or two. Or three.

I play in short bursts of an hour or two and I keep showing them the appetites. Maybe I call over the boss to meet my attractive girl friend and mention with a wink, "Hey, we're going to run up and take a little rest. I told Angel here that you guys have the last Robinson-Basilio fight on film . . . did I ever tell you I won $30,000 on that fight? Would you mind showing it on the closed circuit while we rest? Oh. I'm a couple thousand ahead right now, but I'll just take the chips so I can play later."

They understand me well and they almost pity me, though there is no sign of it at all. They know I had to mention that the girl they were drooling over is going to the room with me. I'm going to impress her with the TV bit. They might remember that the first time I told the $30,000 win story the price was $5,000. They know that I said I was a few thousand ahead, but my markers show I'm $8,000 down. They let me get my stories on.

They understand me, I'm hungry. And the store is mine.

Party: I used to declare myself like that and get all I could. I got so I couldn't stand the pressure of all those backslappers and all those people just "casually" studying my play. I was lucky I had enough put aside to take a year off and let everyone forget me as a high roller. Now I play $25 chips at the most. I can take the cat-and-mouse at that level.

Mrs. Ms.: Frankly, I don't like to play anything but $5 chips. I don't like the attention even $25 chips cause, and I don't like the idea of having my money fluctuate $1,000 during those occasional plays when things go wild.

Grinder: That's important—you have to play at a comfortable financial and psychological level. That's especially true for newcomers. Modern conditions are tough enough to occupy your attention without the additional worry of playing over your head under circumstances you're not comfortable with.

Author: For instance. . . .

Grinder: Take the tendency towards faster play. The casinos have decided that's a good method to keep people from figuring too much, so they keep a pretty rapid pace if they can. Of course, they also do it because they generally make more money if they deal more hands, but fast dealing can be unnerving as the devil when you're just learning to beat the game.

Party: Yeah, but with a little practice, *you* make more money the faster they deal.

Hungry: Many innovations they've tried in an effort to stop counters end up working to your advantage when you have a powerful system you can use easily in action. Multiple decks are a good example.

Grinder: Multiples were supposed to stop all counters . . . and just about did. In Nevada, there's a continuing trend towards using multiples and, of course, most other places in the world use them exclusively. Many casino owners *love* multiples for two reasons: one, they give the house another third to a half a percent advantage; and two, most system players can't beat multiples.

From a playing standpoint, multiples give fewer favorable situations than single decks, and your advantage for various Exact Counts is slightly less. These factors are partially balanced by the fact that favorable situations tend to last longer when they do occur.

Party: They're the greatest, though. No one watches multiples nearly as close as single decks, and you can get down a bigger betting spread. So even though you start out with a little the worst of it, you end up getting the money with hardly any more work. And not nearly as much cat-and-mouse.

Hungry: It's always nice to use casino safeguards to your own advantage. Interestingly, the best possible game to play against is one which combines the most innovations to stop counters: the multiple deck, face-up Blackjack game. Look at the features. All

---

Book Review: Blackjack Gold

Lance Humble's book is needlessly flawed by excessive pre-occupation with cheating, as well as some strange notions about how to maneuver through the world of winning Blackjack play.

Otherwise, the book offers a nice package of interesting information. The system presented is mathematically a winner.

Humble also offers advanced systems for sale at around the $200 mark. These are as good as the best systems which have previously been offered to the general public. Our Special Report on Blackjack Systems gives all the details for those interested in bottom-line comparison.

Humble has also started a Blackjack Club, members of which are polled and in effect "trade" information.

Humble has made an honest attempt at offering prospective Blackjack players a well-rounded package of winning information. He succeeds to a remarkable degree.

---

cards are dealt face up, except the dealer's hole card. That means you can keep an almost completely accurate count at all times. No one usually touches the cards except the dealer. That means the customers can't fiddle with the cards and stall and peek and act like they're playing poker instead of 21. Thus, the game goes very fast, with the dealer pressing everyone for quick decisions. That means you get many more hands per hour.

The net result is that Nevada casinos hope face-up games will catch on, because they make more profit as hands are dealt faster, and because they have the higher multiple deck percentage in their favor. Also, they're about convinced that system players can't keep up with it.

Grinder: It's just a shame the general public hasn't taken a liking to it in Nevada. You can make more money against *that* game than any other style game the casinos have come up with, given the Master *or* the Expert System. Granted, it's a tough game if you have a weak or rigid system, but. . . .

Mrs. Ms.: It's funny how every time we start talking about some particular aspect of system play, the subject gets back to system strength and flexibility.

Styles: Mrs. Ms.

I guess the major components of my style are that money is of no consequence and I am always killing time. It's usually not long after I sit down that I'm engaged in conversation with either the dealer or another player. This is a very pleasant way to pass the time. People are very interesting and will reveal the most wonderful things about themselves with strangers who they never expect to see again. It's a very nice bonus.

Other than that, I never go out of my way to be tricky or deceptive. I suppose most casino personnel don't have their guard up so much with women, but I really prefer to think of playing as strictly a business endeavor.

It goes like this: No matter how nice they are, or for what reason, they "know" that they have an advantage on every bet you make and that they are going to get your money if you play long enough. Everything else is a side trip, at least to me.

So if they feel that you are going to lose your money eventually, because the house has the edge and you're bucking the odds to begin with, and they still feel that they can look you in the eye and make small talk, what's the harm in playing that side game as well?

What we're all doing is legal, after all. They figure they have the edge, and I figure I have the edge. The cards decide. About once in fourteen plays they decide against me, and when that

(Continued)

Grinder: It has to. When you have both, it becomes a challenge to see what the casinos will dream up next to stop counters. Something changes, you make a small adjustment, and you just keep making money.

Hungry: That is really where it's at. As long as it doesn't take much energy to overcome their nonsense, you can sit back and enjoy the game. You're riding easy with a powerful system which doesn't take all your attention, so you crack a joke or two to loosen everyone up and pretty soon they see you're not *serious* about winning and you're obviously not paying too much attention to anything. You're there for a good time, a few laughs, a little unwinding at stakes that make it interesting for everyone.

Styles: **Mrs. Ms.** (Con't.)

happens it makes me glad to know that I've given them about the same sporting chance as they give the average player.

As for betting, I bet almost strictly in proportion to my advantage (chapter 4) with $5 chips and use about a 1 to 8 betting spread, so long as I don't have to increase more than two or three units at a time. As a result, my money fluctuates very little and I almost always win in a half an hour or forty-five minutes. That's the span that seems to look about right for killing time.

I'm not very good at math, but I do know every decision possible in the Expert System. Since I began playing five years ago, my earning rate has always been right around $100 an hour, a fact which infuriates Grinder—his computer program says no one is supposed to be able to do that well at my level of play.

I've never seriously considered moving up to higher action because I'm very content to stay anonymous, because I feel I'm already inordinately rewarded for the "work" I do, and because I think at any higher level the amount of money going back and forth creates too much tension.

I really enjoy what I do. After health, the first independence is economic, and the second is having unobligated time to enjoy. There are literally billions of people in the world who have not been—and will never be—as fortunate as I am in being able to enjoy both.

Now, when they buy *that,* you really get the kind of game you want. All the tension leaves everyone. You can have the game fast or slow or any way you like. Maybe you start winning and the bosses take to sweating (watching closely) the game. Great. You call them in close, by name, and announce laughingly that soon they're going to be working for you. Meantime, you slow the pace down drastically as you're kidding around. Pow . . . they vanish. They know they're never going to get the money back if you don't play a lot of hands. You go back to business as usual.

Party: You guys pull off that high-roller, good 'ol boy routine pretty good. The last time I saw you on the Strip you were handing the casino manager a string of fish you'd caught in a boat he loaned you, and giving him instructions on how you wanted the gourmet room to cook them. That's unreal.

Hungry: When you know you can adjust easily, and when you know you have a strong and flexible system which is going to win for you, there's no reason not to have fun as you go.

Mrs. Ms.: You guys are off to the moon again with that high-roller act. Most people would be interested in, say, how to overcome the early shuffle more than how to get the casino manager's boat.

Grinder: Okay, okay. Everyone sweats the dealer shuffling. That's because they have systems which don't locate enough favorable situations, so they have to chunk out a bunch in the few good situations that are located. You don't have nearly the problem with the Expert or the Master Systems. But early shuffling has knocked out most system players.

The joke of it all is that even Thorp demonstrated back in 1966 that he could win with his system if they dealt one hand. So how the heck are they going to stop *us?*

Hungry: Sure; in the old days they dealt all the way through and a five year old baboon could win against that. It's not the same any more. What with the early shuffle, and all the other aggravations, you're lucky to make $1500 an hour or so.

The bright side, though, is that they've cut us back about as much as they can with that early shuffle. With the power we have now, they'll drive all their customers away before they can stop us.

Party: Maybe you guys love it, but I don't. It seems to me that just about every time the deck gets really good, it's time to shuffle.

Grinder: Sure, that's exasperating. If they'd deal through, we'd about triple our hourly rate. You also wouldn't be able to get a seat to play, what with all the meatball system players in action again. So, you anticipate the shuffle point and don't get caught with your big bet out, and you keep playing little betting games with the dealer so he doesn't shuffle any sooner than he normally would. That, naturally, is how you do it with the anonymous bit. If you play large enough, and shuck 'em enough, you can get them to do pretty much what you'd like. For newcomers, though, having a dealer shuffle early can be unnerving.

Mrs. Ms.: If a dealer does start shuffling sooner, he's really

---

Book Review: **Turning the Tables on Las Vegas**

Ian Anderson's book puts everyone on a bit, but the underlying principles of play are sound indeed. The Anderson style is flamboyant, an effective technique at the high roller level of play.

Must reading, especially if you're a little rusty in the personality, public relations and style department. Keep in mind that this is probably not the best technique for "low-rollers." Notoriety comes too quickly.

Fun and recommended reading . . . with a pinch of salt.

---

telling you something. You have to figure out what it is without asking.

Party: Yeah, it's an argument you can't win if you beef about a dealer's right to shuffle. You call a lot of attention to yourself and you might not really change anything.

Hungry: That's generally true. One thing he might be telling you is that his pit boss is from the old superstition school and likes to see dealers shuffle when a customer gets on a winning streak—break a bad run of cards, and all that.

Grinder: If that's the case, the dealer is likely to shuffle when you have a big bet out if you seem to be winning most of the hands. That has nothing to do with the possibility of his suspecting system play.

Party: I go along with that—most dealers don't know much, but like to put up a sharp front. I caught another guy last week who shuffled every time I put my big bet out. I always figure that's a sign to mosey on, but I tested him first. Sure enough, he'd shuffle when the deck game me a big *disadvantage* as long as I lumped a stack of chips out there. I just kept letting him shuffle away those bad decks. I got him for $500 in less than an hour betting $25 chips, with no one the wiser. So for being a smart guy, he got to watch me leave without giving him a toke (gambling jargon for "token of appreciation," or "tip").

Hungry: *That* can be what a shuffle-happy dealer is telling you—that you're winning and not toking, and he's going to break your run of cards.

Grinder: If you use a little judgment, a quick shuffle almost never means the dealer is counting the deck, though a few might notice an obvious situation . . . such as all the fives coming out on the first hand. If you do find a dealer who shuffles when the deck is favorable to players, and who deals through when it's unfavorable, that's really a form of cheating for the house. *Of course, then the house has to worry about the dealer using a little creative shuffling to help his friends.*

Hungry: Once in a great while you find dealers who can count, using some simplistic system or other. They can be overcome because they can't locate all favorable situations the Expert or, especially, the Master Count does, much less have an accurate playing strategy. But why bother? There are so many easier games around.

Party: Any dealer who could keep track well enough to catch a really good player would be out playing himself and making a ton. I think most dealers who learn some count or other use it for a toke hustle. They catch some guy using a gross system and say, "How's the system working, sir?" Then they expect a big toke for having caught on. Right, Pit Boss?

Author: I can't really go along with that one. The vast majority of dealers never even try to learn any kind of count. They're pretty busy at the table just adding cards and making correct payoffs, and very few are willing to work any harder than they think they already do.

As for the toke hustle, that'll get a dealer fired. In the strictest sense, allowing someone to play who might have a viable system is a form of collusion. It's true that dealers hustle tokes all the time, but not generally in a way which would jeopardize their jobs. A dealer likes to give the impression of being a disinterested third party in a contest between players and Lady Luck, but he really identifies with the house, because that's where his job security is. And no dealer would like the reputation of having a table full of system players all the time because he was considered "easy."

When it comes down to it, what a dealer likes best is for customers to start winning early, toke a bunch, and then lose a bundle. That way, the bosses are happy the house is winning, and the dealer is happy to get a piece of it. The dealer likes it especially well

---

The Team Scheme

Theoretically, the team approach to playing Blackjack appears very attractive. The basic idea is that a gang of Small Bettors count down decks all over a casino while a Big Bettor or two roams about awaiting signals to plunk down monster bets when favorable situations occur.

Imagine: Small Bettor on Table 3 signals the deck is great. Big Bettor saunters over and . . . SMASHO! Here comes a maximum bet. And another. And another, until the deck becomes unfavorable again. Big Bettor casually leaves to roam about until he gets another signal, maybe this time from Table 12, or 7, or 26.

It seems almost perfect. Big Bettor cannot be counting cards. He makes big bets only, all over the place and apparently on impulse. Hunch-happy and maybe even "drunk," he looks just like the standard whippy compulsive, right?

Wrong. It's an old wheeze used and abused to the point that casinos are very much on guard against it (read Ken Uston's, The Big Player).

That doesn't mean that all team play is unproductive. Given some clever application, deception and a little variation from the expected, team play can be productive indeed.

Unfortunately, the best, most sophisticated and viable of these techniques are for the present proprietary and beyond the scope of this book. But maybe later. . . .

---

if that whole scenario happens quickly so he can fold his arms and not deal for awhile.

Party: You're right about that. Dealers are a lazy lot. All they want is for you to hurry up and get broke so they can stand around and do nothing. Can you imagine what would happen if dealers were allowed to bar anyone? They'd claim everyone who didn't toke was a system player. It's that simple.

Author: It's unfortunate, but too many dealers begin to fit into a well-defined mold after awhile, and lazy is a big part of it. It's understandable, in a way, since what they do is dull and repetitious, and not very meaningful. Can you imagine standing on your feet adding up cards and settling bets year after year? It might be interesting at first, but after awhile you'd begin to feel—if not act—like a robot. On the other hand, the money is great, considering the average dealer's qualifications for any other kind of work.

Another part of the mold is resentment. Besides resenting the tedium, a dealer feels he's always in the middle. When customers lose, they abuse him, and when the house loses the bosses sometimes act like it's his fault.

He comes to resent the players who make him do his robot work. You might think dealing would be an interesting job, because the dealer meets new people all the time. But all he sees are different faces making the same comments about the same hands day after day after day. He deals thousands and thousands of hands to hundreds and hundreds of players every week and it begins to be the same thing for him for as far back as he can remember and as far ahead as he can imagine because the money is too good to ever consider doing anything else.

There are exceptions, a lot of them. Some go into another line of work which is more satisfying. The ones who stay and maintain a pleasant outlook are exceptions, indeed.

Now, back to dealers counting. Most of them only do exactly what is expected of them; they shuffle up if someone is obvious enough about betting or playing to get their attention. They wouldn't do that if they weren't trying to impress the bosses and keep their jobs.

As you know, I've worked with hundreds of dealers. A few of them were awake enough to point out to me on occasion that they thought a particular customer was a system player. Without exception, the dealers were right. Also without exception, the customer in question did *not* have a system that could win in the long run. It's really the same thing with dealers as with pit bosses; if you play as they think system players play, they suspect you whether you're capable or not, because they really don't know.

Grinder: In the end, I don't think it makes much difference what a dealer *or* a pit boss knows or doesn't know. If you play a strong system and use a little judgment, there really isn't much for them to latch onto. Of course, they're going to watch if you start winning a lot; keeping an eye on the house bankroll is part of their job. Mostly, though, there just isn't enough about your play to hold their attention.

Hungry: You also never give them anything to worry about when you know they're *really* paying attention.

Party: They all take a look once in awhile, but if you don't seem to be doing anything when they do, they've got to go to sleep. And, if you're a woman, you don't have to take *any* precautions. . . .

Mrs. Ms.: That's not entirely true, but it is true that casino personnel hardly ever pay attention to the way women bet. I usually bet strictly in proportion to my advantage and maintain somewhere between a one-to-six, or maybe eight, betting spread with single decks. No one seems to pay much attention.

Party: That's because they all keep their heads full of clever things to say so they can try to make time. . . .

Mrs. Ms.: That's where disadvantages come in for women. Someone is always trying to carry on a conversation, just to be nice. Some dealers and players still act as if an unescorted woman is an easy target, but most just think a woman is less interested in playing and would like to talk. That's distracting.

Hungry: I think any woman has much more potential for winning than a man, because no one thinks a woman able to handle a system. For some reason, that just happens to be true—I've tried to teach two wives and at least a half-dozen traveling companions, and they've all been washouts.

Mrs. Ms.: That's because most women are indoctrinated from birth not to think for themselves. You get the right information to the right women nowadays, and you'll *see* some winners. That's really *my* reason for being willing to give out any information about playing Blackjack—I'd like to see other gals get in on a good thing.

Grinder: Then why don't you tell them your theory about Countertactics? It would be helpful to men, too.

Mrs. Ms.: It might be something women have a better feel for. In its simplest sense, Countertactics just means the intelligent use of options all players have. For instance, you can choose the casino, the shift and the time you want to play. Also, you can choose the rules and conditions carefully before you sit down. You can leave a table on a high minus count; you can go back to places where you feel most capable and comfortable.

Eventually, you begin to realize the way you act itself is a Countertactic, an option you can use to your advantage. The way you buy in, play, bet, act, look, cash out . . . all those things tell casino personnel you are maybe rich, poor, friendly, calculating, dependent, bored, stupid, anxious, puzzled, etc.—anything but a scientific player.

Pretty soon you find the right combination and they deal a little deeper; they don't pay attention to a little bigger betting spread; they don't notice you sitting there a little longer.

Finally, you discover that the original Countertactics of worrying about the best rules and all that doesn't really matter beyond the fact that you must make a slight adjustment in your very adjustable system. After that, it becomes mostly a matter of putting in time and cashing out money.

Grinder: That might be the best place to end this discussion. You play a solid system, get experience, a feel for the game, and you gain confidence. When you have all that, the ups and downs of the short run don't seem as significant. You just grind 'em up and keep cashing out chips.

THE LAST WORD—BETWEEN YOU AND ME

Well, that's about it—some dynamite information from some very successful people.

I hope you enjoyed it. Better than that, I hope you make a great deal of money using the Expert System.

Let me ask a favor. When you start winning, drop me a card—anonymously if you prefer—and tell me about it. I'd like to think I've pulled off one of the coups of this Century by being able to reveal the fantastically-powerful Expert System. Nowhere have I found anyone audacious enough to print a system proven so powerful by computer, *and actually played for extended time by professionals who weren't barred for using it.* And further, published the system while it was at the peak of its power.

So take the information and run! It's super solid. It's proven. It works. It really works! You should be able to capture many a ton with it, and with no one the wiser.

It'll be especially gratifying to me if you do. You wouldn't believe the number of losers I've seen in casinos. But you also couldn't guess the amount of satisfaction I'd find in thinking I might be a bit responsible for changing some of those frowns to smiles.

So do me that favor. Drop a card in care of the publisher and let me know how you're doing. You can be brief, if you like. In fact, just draw a picture of a happy face if the Expert System is especially good for you.

See, I always wanted to make a mark in this gambling world, where I've spent so much time.

That happy face would be the best mark of all!

The fox has *many* tricks . . .

Erasmus

The Last Word

Getting it on better,
faster, bigger

If you've read the previous material closely, you're now in a most unusual position: you know, perhaps, more about winning at the game of Blackjack than any other *single* individual has ever known before publication of this book. I hope the information is very lucrative for you, indeed.

If you're interested in going even further, or want more information, here's the way to do it:

ADVANCED BASIC MODIFICATIONS FOR THE EXPERT SYSTEM

This book, *Blackjack Your Way to Riches*, contains all the details and refinements for the Expert System that *most* players will ever need.

However, if you plan playing a great deal, or simply want the maximum power and bucks you can possibly gain from the Expert System every time you play, you will find further modifications for the Basic Strategy helpful. Here's why.

You remember that using the Basic Strategy as it appears in this book is the way you will play most of the time. You also remember that, depending on the composition of the remaining cards in the deck, you sometimes deviate from Basic as to how you play certain hands.

For instance, at a count of +5, you learned in chapter 5 that you would stand with a total of 16 in your hand against a dealer's upcard of 9, even though Basic Strategy told you to hit. Your count and modified playing strategy has told you that you have more going for you by standing than hitting at that particular count with that particular hand.

All of the modifications to the Basic Strategy that you will ever make with counts that range from +6 to −6 are already in your hands in this book.

But there are additional modifications possible. These are called for less frequently; but when they are, they can add significantly to the Expert System's strength.

For instance, knowing the exact point at which *you do not split Aces* against a dealer's upcard 6 can not only save you the additional money you would put up for splitting, but might very well enable you to play and very possibly win with the Aces you would otherwise have split.

In all, there are more than 80 decisions which come into play above +6 and below −6. They tell you when it is wiser not to split eights against a 9, when you should *not* double down with 11 against an upcard 5, and many other extraordinary plays which put a razor edge on your Expert System. Sometimes, the difference of just one of these plays can swing the balance from loss to profit on a given play.

To order, see the last page of this book.

SPECIAL REPORT ON BLACKJACK SYSTEMS

This is one of the most eye-opening, valuable and interesting sources of information anyone interested in Blackjack could ever own. *The Special Report on Blackjack Systems* analyzes, summarizes and compares all of the most popular Blackjack systems now on the market. Tells in detail how to separate good systems from bad; how systems are constructed; what system strengths and weaknesses are. Absolutely ends all arguments as to which systems are poor, good, better and best . . . and why. After reading this, you will know more about card-counting systems than the vast majority of players and casino personnel even suspect.

In addition, the *Special Report on Blackjack Systems* reveals how some mail order system sellers operate to bilk the public with systems which cost all the way up to $200 and more, and how they get endorsements for their systems.

This Special Report also tells which of the current systems are viable, and exactly how good they are both mathematically and practically. (Not all systems are bad or impractical, but many of them have dubious value.) Gives you all the information you need to make up your mind about most available systems.

This Special Report is written informally enough for general understanding, but also includes enough solid math to solidly substantiate all data. Includes mathematical and practical information on: simplistic counts, ten-counts, point counts, plus-minus counts, complex point counts, multi-parameter counts, an analysis of the Expert Count and a discussion of the Master Count.

In addition, there are sections on the effect of betting spread to profit, and the effects of correction for Aces. Also, a formula for determining the average profit available in terms of any basic betting unit, and an explanation and formulae for both playing efficiency and betting efficiency. Finally, you will discover why mathematicians often fail at system invention, as do players who attempt invention without a math background (it takes both).

If you are interested in Blackjack, you will find this information enlightening; if you are playing—or planning to play—*any* system, you *need* this Special Report. It could save you hundreds, perhaps thousands, of dollars.

To order, see the last page of this book.

THE MASTER SYSTEM

I saved the absolute best for the absolute last.

You recall that several times during the course of this book I mentioned there is one practical system in all the world more powerful in actual play than the Expert System you now have in your hands. That more powerful system is the Master System, and I promised you'd have a chance to purchase it if it met your needs.

However, let me re-state an important series of facts. The Expert System, which you purchased in this book, is the most powerful simple and practical system which has ever been offered to the public at any price! There's none better, therefore, *except* the Master System.

If you've read this far, I'll have to assume you really want everything there is to have out of playing Blackjack: the maximum amount of money in the shortest possible time; the most money for the smallest bankroll you wish to risk; the least worry of playing like other system players.

You get all that with the Master System, but let me warn you about the conditions of sale:

1) *My contributors decide how many will be sold, and to whom.*

2) *They can withdraw from the offer of selling anytime they wish, no matter how* few *have been sold.* (They simply don't want their action hurt with excessive competition.)

You can see we're not interested in selling a lot of Master Systems. Let me give you a few personal observations that might help you decide if the Master System is for you.

I'd say, you *might* need the Master System if:

. . . You're an experienced player, you already know all the ins and outs of the game, you definitely *know* Blackjack is for you, and you want to move right to the top in power.

. . . You know you want to have the maximum power you can have at some time in the future, and you don't want to "unlearn" one system in order to advance and "relearn" the Master System.

. . . You're like Grinder and Hungry, and you want the most you can possibly have going for you anytime you play.

Now, you *might* need the Master System if you fit into any of those catagories, but you definitely *do not* need the Master System if you fit into any of these:

. . . You have never played the game. (The Expert System you already have will give you all the power you need for openers.)

. . . You are only going to play a few hours a year. (No sense going to any more trouble or expense than using the Expert System you already have, which is almost as likely to show the same profit in very short runs. Plus, why take a Master System out of circulation which someone could get full-time use of?)

. . . You are planning on playing dollars only. (Using the Master System for that kind of play would be like using an elephant gun to shoot squirrel.)

If you're still reading, let me add some additional information which might help you decide. The Expert System you have already purchased is considered "simple" because it counts the relative value of cards as they are removed from the deck by employing either $+1$, -1, or 0. Given the playing strategy, all of the possible power that can be extracted from the game using those values is incorporated in the Expert System.

Now, the Master System does not use those values. Its counting system values cards more perfectly in proportion to their effect as they are removed from the deck. Thus, the Master System is somewhat more difficult than the Expert System.

This increased difficulty is more than compensated for by increased earning power . . . *if you can handle it.* In other words, given the additional power, you might be hitting in a given situation where the Expert System would call for standing, or doubling with the Master System where the Expert System told you to simply hit. The Master System would be more correct in these, and many other close situations, because it's more accurate. Therefore, you wouldn't need as much bankroll for a given betting spread, and you wouldn't need as big a betting spread for the same win rate.

Let's talk a little further about Master System advantages. First, it has a higher mathematical expectation than *any* other practical system on the market, proved out by computer and actual play by Grinder, Hungry and myself. As I told you, I can't play too much in too many places because of my reputation of being "sharp," but among the three of us we've logged over a decade of actual playing time with the Master System at very sweet rates. Mrs. Ms. and Party are still using the Expert System.

In dollar expectation, my contributors supplied the following to indicate how much per hour the Master System meant in *increased* income over the Expert System.

For Grinder, increased income per hour jumped up about $300 over the Expert System.

For Hungry, increased income jumped up about $250 an hour.

As you know, those two play strictly $100 chips.

That should give you a ball-park kind of idea of what the Master System can mean in dollar return. However, this is a good time to repeat what you no doubt already know, having read chapter 6: my contributors know exactly what they're doing and are able to get the most out of every situation. Now, even if you are experienced, your actual increase in income over the Expert System will vary and depend upon many things, including your betting spread, how well you play, the size units you bet, how many players in the game, etc., etc., etc.

What I can absolutely state unequivocally, is that the mathematical expectation is there and has been realized consistently in actual play. It should definitely work for you. But here's a warning: if you can't handle the increased difficulty of the Master System, you would probably make more money playing the Expert System.

I should by now have discouraged most readers from getting too interested in the Master System. That's good. For not only is the Master System expensive, but not every one can have one even if he can afford it.

Now, for those of you who are still curious enough to hang in there, I'm going to tell you some of the more positive aspects of the Master System without reservation. It took me about eight hours to learn it. After testing it extensively for about six months, I found it to be truly a work of art. By "art," I mean simply that it has all of the seven elements of a perfect system incorporated into one harmonious whole:

1. *It locates favorable situations as accurately as possible. You know the amount of your advantage or disadvantage at all times more completely than with any other viable system.*

2. *It is extremely powerful, effective and deceptive against either single or multiple decks.*

3. *With a little practice, it is so logical and smooth in use that you can play for hours with no fatigue.*

4. *It is not as difficult to learn or to apply as more complex counts, yet still produces a greater return.*

5. *It combines all the superior elements of the best existing theoretical and practical techniques into one extremely efficient method of play.*

6. *It has been tested in actual play for about a decade (combining all our time with it), and this play has borne out its mathematical expectation as predicted by computer.*

7. *The House cannot prevent the Master System player from winning except by refusing to allow him to play!*

If I sound as if I've become enthralled by the Master System, I guess I have to admit it. When you know what Blackjack is all about, and you have the experience, you can really appreciate this incredibly smooth-functioning gem.

Because of this, you can appreciate how my contributors must insist upon protecting the Master System, and restricting it from general use in every way possible. Sale of the Master System will be strictly limited. In that regard, give a listen to Grinder, the spokesman for my contributors:

"We don't mind sharing a little if there's enough profit in it for us. However, there are realistic limits as to how many Master System players the game can stand. Also, we don't need excessive competition.

"Therefore, at the exact point we believe that the game might be hurt, or that our own ability to make money might be impaired, by further sale of the Master System, we reserve the right to withdraw the offer of selling the Master System. We reserve the right that our judgment be the sole determinant in this matter."

There you have it, the protection, the stipulations, the conditions, and the guarantees. Now the bad news.

It's expensive. And here's Grinder again to tell you what you already know:

"It's supposed to hurt; this is an exclusive club. We weren't going to let out any at all, at first. But we finally decided a prohibitive price would give us a little built-in protection, besides profit. Someone who's willing to put up a sizable chunk of money is very likely to be very sure of what he or she is doing and perhaps be a little more willing to exercise judgment and care as to protecting his investment, protecting the system, and protecting the game."

Now, here's an exact rundown as to what you get for the money:

1. The complete Master System my contributors use today; nothing left out, nothing held back. If there are any further refinements to the Master System (such as adapting to some oddball rule some future casino might adopt), they will be sent to you upon request without charge.

2. A free *Special Report on Blackjack Systems,* which gives the precise mathematical and practical information to evaluate all of the popular systems offered today. (See previous description.) You're entitled to know why you're King of the Mountain.

3. The right to ask a reasonable number of any kind of questions you might have, and have them answered by return mail.

I think you'll agree that this is quite a package. Oh! You'll be

happy to know that purchasing the Master System doesn't necessi-
tate re-learning large blocks of material you've already read in
Blackjack Your Way to Riches. In fact, the two complement each
other, and using the Master System assumes you have reached the
level of sophistication that *Blackjack Your Way to Riches* guides
you to.

Well that's about it, an extraordinary opportunity. It's prohibitive in price, but I truly envy those of you who can afford it and
can get one before anything happens to the offer. You should be
virtually unstoppable.

To order, see the last page of this book.

ABOVE AND BEYOND THE SCOPE OF THIS BOOK

Blackjack Your Way to Riches *contains information which is the highest quality, the most comprehensive and the most effective of any on Blackjack which has ever been published. It's good enough to make even an amateur rich if he follows the program.*

No one else has ever had the knowledge or has been confident enough to make that statement.

That doesn't mean that this is all there is to know about legitimate winning techniques, however. There's much, much more: super-sophisticated math techniques undreamed of by the math profs, ultra-keen procedural techniques unsuspected by insiders or outsiders, and technology-enhanced perceptual techniques unimagined by the sharpest of the sharp. And more. Much, much more.

Some, but not all, of these apply to Blackjack. Some apply to other casino games. Some are even outside the area of casino gaming. All get the money, legitimately and honestly. All depend upon having superior information and using that information effectively.

If there proves to be sufficient interest in these areas, some of these topics may be the subject of future offerings from Expertise Publishing Company.

If it sounds interesting, make sure your name is on the publisher's mailing list. You're a winner with Expertise.

APPENDICES

Appendix A

The Ultra, Super, Dynamite, Razzamatazz Refinements to Expert Basic Strategy

It is possible to make a few changes in your Expert Basic Strategy and extract a teeny-tiny bit more power when playing against various numbers of decks. These changes might be worthwhile if:

1. You have no intention of ever learning to keep track of cards AND

2. You *only* play against two decks, or, say, four decks.

3. You have a good memory and can switch decisions against different numbers of decks.

Otherwise, make it easy on yourself and stick to the Expert Basic Strategy presented in chapter 2.

Should you suspect that this is a kind of flip-lip approach to what appears to be a serious concern to the outside amateurs, here's some details.

Expert Basic Strategy tells you the best possible way to play your two cards against any dealer upcard, without taking into consideration any other cards. It was computed, balanced and weighted to give the best possible average play in *all* situations *where no other cards are known.*

Better plays beyond that should be tied to the Expert Count and system of play, if you want the most return for your dollar. That is, unless the above three exceptions apply.

It's really a question of energy expended for dollars gained. It might sound clever to memorize a lot of changes to Expert Basic for play against different numbers of decks, but the result for all that work amounts to pennies. Spend the energy on the Expert Count and measure your return in megabucks.

197

There are many fallacies involved in the logic of memorizing, say, a four-deck Basic to play against a four-deck shoe. For in reality, that Basic is only "accurate" in play against the fourth deck to the third deck. Then the player should switch to a three-deck basic, and so forth.

And here's the kicker: all of the possible Basics depend upon a normal distribution of cards to the nearest deck. That's unlikely through all of the decks, to be sure.

Let's carry it one step further.

Did you know that Basic should change at the 3½ deck level? And at the 2⅛ deck level? And at the 1¼ deck level. And. . . .

Yes, it changes all the time. But if you try to account for those changes without keeping track of cards, you're always assuming card distribution is normal and that your Basic is therefore correct. A great deal of the time it won't be exactly correct. Why try and make Basic do what a card-counting system is supposed to do?

The solution to the problem is to use Expert Basic Strategy against all decks, and when ready for it, employ the Expert Count to modify Basic decisions as cards are dealt (see chapter 5). In any case, without the Expert Count you aren't likely to know when you have the advantage and when to bet more.

Further, all the possible Basic modifications you can commit to memory aren't going to overcome the following house advantage figures:

1 deck game	.015%
2 deck game	.34%
4 deck game	.50% (half a percent)
6 deck game	.60%
60 deck game	.66%
6,000 deck game	.68%

So, if you're going to go to any trouble past Expert Basic Strategy, put your efforts into the Expert Count which *will* overcome the house edge against you by both maximizing your betting and by enabling you to modify Basic with extreme accuracy no matter how many decks you play against or how far they're depleted. Again, see chapter 5 for details.

For those of you who would still like to have the changes, here they are:

Two-Deck Changes

Player's Hand	Dealer's Upcard	Change From Basic Strategy
8-3, 9-2	Ace	Hit, instead of doubling.
Ace-3	4	Hit, instead of doubling.
Ace-6	2	Hit, instead of doubling.
Ace-7	A	Hit, instead of standing.
6-6	2	Hit, instead of splitting.
2-2	3	Hit, instead of splitting.

Four-Deck Changes

All of the above two-deck changes apply to four or more decks with the following additional changes.

Do not double any 11 versus a dealer's upcard Ace; hit, instead.

Do not double 9 versus a dealer's upcard 2; hit, instead.

Appendix B

Expectation, Fluctuation and Probability of Success

Expectation, fluctuation and probability of success are intricately related and all tough to analyze. That's because they are subject to most of the variables listed in chapter 4 (betting spread, bankroll, rules, how well you play, shuffle point, etc. etc.).

Experienced players nail these critters down cold by keeping careful records over a period of time which relate specifically to the way they play and under what conditions.

However, by assuming certain constants, you can make some estimates helpful in understanding a few of the deeper mysteries of Blackjack system play. Let's take a look at some details.

One way to measure your chance of success should be through the probability (in percent) of *doubling* your bankroll before you might have the misfortune of losing your bankroll. Your chance of success depends upon two factors:

1. The number of units in your bankroll.

2. The *average* percent you have in your favor with the system you use. This figure depends upon,

• betting spread—the greater the spread, the greater the percent in your favor.

• shuffle point—the deeper they go the better it is for you.

• number of players in the game—the fewer the better.

• level of expertise you've achieved with your system.

• decks in use—singles are better than doubles, doubles are better than four decks, etc.

Now we'll make the assumptions. Let's say for a moment you are using the Expert Count with Basic Strategy only, you usually play against a single deck (but sometimes play against doubles), you often play with other players in the game, and you use a 1 to 4 betting spread. What are your chances of doubling your bankroll before losing it?

According to chapter 4, "Money Management," you should have at least a Total Bankroll of 120 units. We suggested 200 units would be safer. Here's why:

Expert Count With Basic Strategy Decisions

Total Bankroll	Chance of Doubling Before Losing Entire Bankroll
200 units	88%
120 units	77%
100 units	73%
60 units	65%
50 units	63%
40 units	60%
20 units	56%

But now let's assume you're playing the Expert Count and have incorporated the Advanced Expert Techniques (chapter 5) into your play. Here are your chances:

Expert Count Using Advanced Expert Techniques

Total Bankroll	Chance of Doubling Before Losing Entire Bankroll
200 units	98%
120 units	90%
100 units	88%
60 units	77%
50 units	74%
40 units	69%
20 units	60%

Notice that the odds of losing any amount are predicated on *doubling* that amount, and that the odds of losing drop in direct proportion to the size of your bankroll.

Therefore, if you increase the size of your Total Bankroll as you are winning, you can all but eliminate your chances of losing your entire bankroll. The odds will be the same at the outset, but you can change them as you increase your bankroll.

For instance, say you start with a Total Bankroll of 120 units, and you're playing all the Advanced Expert Techniques. After five times out, you've won 80 units. You add that to your original bankroll.

In that case, where at the outset you had a 10% chance of losing the 120 units before winning 120 units, you now have only a 2% chance of losing 200 units before winning 200 units. If you keep adding the small wins to your total Bankroll until you have acquired 400 units, your chance of losing that whole amount before doubling the 400 units are virtually the same as your being hit by a comet.

While fluctuations of 10 to 20 top bets are predictable in the short run, fluctuations of a magnitude great enough to wipe out your Total Bankroll are extraordinary, and to the percentage figure named.

Here's some further interesting observations you can make from the above charts.

A player using Advanced Expert Techniques has twice the advantage over the house as a player using the Expert Count strictly with Basic Strategy.

Therefore, if you double your advantage, you only need one half the bankroll to have the same chance of success:

Expert Count with Basic,
    chances of doubling 200 units .... 88% success

Advanced Expert chances of
    doubling just 100 units .... 88% success

Or, to put it another way, with twice the advantage for any given bankroll, you can bet twice as much and win four times as much with the same chance of success. Example:

Expert with Basic and a 200 unit bankroll, betting *1 to 4*, has an 88% chance of success.

Advanced Expert and a 200 unit bankroll, betting *2 to 8*, has an 88% chance of success.

Betting 2 to 8 with twice the advantage wins *four times* as much money with the same chance of success!

Now for some details on the win-rate chart given in chapter 4, "Money Management." That chart told you a player using the Expert Count with Basic Strategy only should win one top bet or more per hour. And also, that a player using the Advanced Expert Techniques should win two or more top bets an hour. Take a look at these:

Expert Count With Basic Only:
1 to 4 Betting Spread

Hours Played	Number of Expected Top Bet Wins	Chance of Success	Chance of Failure
50	50 (or 200 units)	88%	12%
25	25 (or 100 units)	73%	17%
10	10 (or 40 units)	60%	40%
5	5 (or 20 units)	56%	44%

Advanced Expert Techniques:
1 to 4 Betting Spread

Hours Played	Number of Expected Top Bet Wins	Chance of Success	Chance of Failure
25	50 (or 200 units)	98%	2%
12½	25 (or 100 units)	88%	12%
5	10 (or 40 units)	69%	31%
2½	5 (or 20 units)	60%	40%

You can see that a player using Advanced Expert Techniques wins the same number of units *in half the time* as a player using the Expert Count with Basic only.

Also, that Advanced Expert Techniques win twice as much as the Expert Count with Basic only, in the same time and with a greater chance of success.

Or, the Advanced Expert Techniques can win four times as much as the Expert Count with Basic only, with the same chance of success by doubling the dollar amount of the betting spread ($2 to $8, instead of $1 to $4, for example).

Appendix C

Selected Publications You Might Find Useful for Background

ANDERSON, IAN
  "Turning the Tables on Las Vegas." (Vanguard Press, New York 1976)
ARCHER, JOHN
  "The Archer Method of Winning at 21." (Henry Regnery Co., Chicago 1973)
BALDWIN, CANTEY, MAISEL, MC DERMOTT
  "Playing Blackjack to Win; A New Strategy for the Game of 21." (M. Barrows & Company, Inc., New York, 1957)

  "The Optimum Strategy in Blackjack." Journal of the American Statistical Association, Volume 51, 429–439 (1956)
BRAUN, JULIAN H.
  "Comparing the Top Blackjack Systems." Gambling Quarterly, Fall/Winter 1974, pp. 22–23, 54–55.

  "The Development and Analysis of Winning Strategies for the Casino Game of Blackjack." (Julian Braun, Chicago 1974)
COLLVER, DONALD L.
  "Scientific Blackjack and Complete Casino Guide (Arco Publishing Company, Inc., New York, 1966)
EINSTEIN, CHARLES
  "How to Win at Blackjack." (Cornerstone Library, New York 1968, New Edition 1971)
EPSTEIN, RICHARD A.
  "The Theory of Gambling and Statistical Logic." (Academic Press, New York 1967)

GARCIA, FRANK
"Marked Cards and Loaded Dice." (Prentice-Hall, Inc., New York 1962)

GOODMAN, MIKE
"How to Win at Cards, Dice, Races and Roulette." (Holloway House Publishing Company, Los Angeles, 1963)

"Your Best Bet" (Brooke House, Northridge, Calif. 1975)

GORDON, EDWARD
"Optimum Strategy in Blackjack—A New Analysis." Claremont Economic Paper Number 52 (Claremont, California, January 1973)

GRIFFIN, PETER
"Rate of Gain in Player Expectation." Gambling And Society, (Charles Thomas Publishing, Springfield, Illinois 1975)

"Use of Bivariate Normal Approximations to Evaluate Single Parameter Card Counting Systems in Blackjack." Paper presented at Second Annual Conference on Gambling held June 1975, Lake Tahoe, Nevada.

HEATH, DAVID
"Algorithms for Computations of Blackjack Strategies." Paper presented at Second Annual Conference on Gambling, Lake Tahoe, Nevada, June 1975.

ITA, KOKO
"21 Counting Methods to Beat 21" (Gambler's Book Club, Las Vegas, 1976)

NOIR, JACQUES
"Casino Holiday." (Oxford Street Press, Berkely 1970)

REVERE, LAWRENCE
"Playing Blackjack as a Business." (Lawrence Revere, Las Vegas 1966), (Paul Mann Publishing Co., Las Vegas 1971), (Lyle Stewart, New York 1973)

ROBERTS, STANLEY
"Winning Blackjack." (Scientific Research Services, Los Angeles, 1971)

ROUGE ET NOIR, STAFF OF
"Winning at Casino Gambling." (Rouge Et Noir, Inc., Glen Head, New York, 1966, Revised 1975)

SCARNE, JOHN
"Scarne's New Complete Guide to Gambling." Revised edition. (Simon & Schuster, Inc., New York 1974)

THORP, EDWARD O.
"Beat the Dealer." A winning strategy for the game of 21. (Random House, New York 1962)

"Beat the Dealer." New Edition. (Vintage Books, New York 1966)

"Blackjack Systems." Paper presented at the Second Annual Conference on Gambling, Lake Tahoe, Nevada, June 1975.

"A Favorable Strategy for Twenty-One." Proceedings of the National Academy of Sciences, Volume 47, No. 1, pp. 110–112 (1961)

"Fortune's Formula: The Game of Blackjack." Notices of the American Mathematical Society, December 1960 pp. 935–936.

"Optimal Gambling Systems for Favorable Games." Review of the International Statistical Institute, 37-3, 1969, pp. 273–293.

and WALDEN, W. E.
"The Fundamental Theorem of Card Counting." International Journal of Game Theory, Volume 2, 1973, Issue 2.

USTON, KEN *with* RAPOPORT, ROGER
"The Big Player." (Holt, Rinehart & Winston, New York 1977)

WILSON, ALLAN N.
"The Casino Gambler's Guide." Revised Edition. (Harper & Row, New York 1970)

WONG, STANFORD
"Professional Blackjack." Revised edition. (GBC Press, Las Vegas, Nevada, 1977)

Appendix D

Playing Record Forms

PLAYING RECORD

Date	Casino	Shift or Time	No. of Decks No. of players Rules	Playing Time	Win or Loss	Cumulative Time Played	Cumulative Win or Loss	Comments

PLAYING RECORD

Date	Casino	Shift or Time	No. of Decks No. of players Rules	Playing Time	Win or Loss	Cumulative Time Played	Cumulative Win or Loss	Comments

PLAYING RECORD

Date	Casino	Shift or Time	No. of Decks No. of players Rules	Playing Time	Win or Loss	Cumulative Time Played	Cumulative Win or Loss	Comments

ORDER FORM

The following order form has been included for your convenience.

Whether you are pursuing successful Blackjack play as an intriguing hobby, a profitable avocation, or a full time professional endeavor, you'll find the special offerings of Expertise Publishing Company to be of considerable interest and value.

But even if you prefer to order later, be sure and send your name and address now if you'd like to receive additional information of interest to you as it becomes available.

Advanced Basic Modifications for
    the Expert System $25.00

Special Report on Blackjack Systems $15.00

The Master System (includes Special Report
    on Blackjack Systems) $250.00

EXPERTISE PUBLISHING COMPANY
P. O. BOX 1862
RENO, NEVADA 89505

EXPERTISE PUBLISHING COMPANY
P. O. BOX 1862
RENO, NEVADA 89505

Enclosed is $_____. Rush me the following information by First Class Mail.

☐ Advanced Basic Modifications for the Expert System $25.00
☐ Special Report on Blackjack Systems $15.00
☐ The Master System (includes Special Report
    on Blackjack Systems) $250.00
☐ Please place my name on your mailing list to receive
    information on future offerings of Expertise Publishing
    Company.

Name _____

Address _____

City _____ State _____ Zip _____
       (Arizona residents please add 5% sales tax)